ATLANTA LOVE JONES

Carolyn Marie

1

A lot of guys in the ATL don't really believe in real love; mainly because they don't know what it is. I was one of those guys. Love is love, but real love can either make you be really smart or make you go really dumb. But a man like me couldn't tell the difference.

I was born and raised as Jayson Adams in the SWATS of Atlanta, Georgia with the same old story of a black man. With only my mother by my side and a group of friends I called my brothers, life was ordinarily hard. I stepped out of bed every morning and stared into the mirror at the same two dark brown eyes looking back at me. After hitting the shower, I untied the white, black, blue, or red durag from my head and scoped the cornrow design in my hair to see if presentable. Once my teeth were Colgate fresh and the arched bone of my face was shaved clean, I raided my closet to cover my defined, bronze chest with a basketball jersey, my legs with a pair of partially baggy jeans, and my feet with the latest Air Jordans that matched whatever color I'd decided to wear.

That day in June when I woke up I chose to honor Michael Jordan in all red and black before I hit the streets. When I left the one-story bungalow I called my home, I took in the heat of the overzealous sunlight that painted my body. I boarded the patent leather seat in my cotton white, Cadillac Escalade and headed a few blocks away to what we called *The Spot*. This corner was notorious for being a hotspot for drug activity with no evidence found at the scene. And my boys and I made it happen.

Parking my car at the other end of the street, I walked back down to greet my friends, as I did every other day. Jordan was the first one I saw; he had the darkest complexion, so he stood out the most. He was the tall, lanky type and lived his life for nobody but himself. Shawn was next to pound my fist. He was the same brown-skin nigga you would see around every corner with the goatee, brand-named outfit, and massive Timberland boots; and he was never too busy to flaunt flashy jewelry around his strong build.

I came to stand next to the man I knew my entire life. Derek was my closest friend, looking and acting like my own brother, and loyal to me like nobody else had ever been. Even my mama claimed him as her child. It didn't hurt that he had the connection we needed to make this money on a regular basis either. We were the dynamic duo and nothing could interfere with that.

As we discussed plans to party and traded narcotics for cash, it was then that I saw her. She strut her long, golden legs in red and white Air Force One high tops down the sidewalk as if she knew what she was doing to me. Her chestnut brown hair blew away from her heart-shaped face to show off the smoky shade around her diamond eyes. As the sun bounced off her pouty, crimson lips, pieces of her shining locks moved to the curvature of cleavage inside the solid red t-shirt that fit the form of her hourglass figure. My eyes followed her hips from side to side as they seemed to suffocate in the baby blue capri pants encasing her onion behind.

She moved further and further away while I looked over at my friends panting like pit bulls. I wanted to say something to her, so I took two steps forward but felt a tug at my jersey from the back.

"Aye, bro," Derek started. "Where you going?"

"I don't know about you, but I'm about to get at shawty," I answered.

"Man, good luck," he scoffed. I continued on my path, trying to catch her before she got away. Just as she was about to make her way around the corner, I stopped her.

"Aye, sweetheart," I began, just inches behind her head. She swung her body to face me.

"Can I help you?" she said.

"Yes, ma'am. I saw you walking by and I wanted to come talk

2

to you,"

"Really?"

"Yeah, girl. What's your name?"

"Joya," she smiled.

"That's beautiful, Joya, my name is Jayson. I was thinking maybe you can give me your number and we could get to know each other, kick it one day,"

"Why?" she wondered. That really threw me for a loop. What kind of question is that?

"What you mean?" I questioned.

"What exactly would be the purpose? Everything that's worth anything has a purpose and you wouldn't want to jump into anything that would waste your time if you knew there was no point,"

"True. But at the same time, you don't know what could be until you pursue it,"

"That's nice," she nodded. "I like that. Maybe you *can* call me. Let me see your phone." I pulled from deep inside my pocket my iPhone and watched her closely as she entered her number into my phone.

"Call me," she said before turning to walk away.

"I got you," I assured her. I took a deep breath and enjoyed one last look at her from the back. It was strange. Never in my life have I had a somewhat intelligent conversation with a girl. It made me feel even more attracted to her.

I joined my friends with a smirk on my face but quickly left them alone since I was so anxious to do something with Joya. I wasted no time once I got back home, and dialed her number as soon as I fell to the russet, plush couch. Ring after ring I was out of my element feeling more and more nervous. Finally, I had convinced myself she wouldn't pick up, and I almost hung up until I heard her voice.

"Hello," Joya answered.

"Aye, what's up," I said, throwing the phone back to my ear; I put my nerves back in the box and let out my cool.

"Who is this?" she asked.

"Jayson,"

"Oh; you didn't waste any time, did you?"

"Would you? What you doing, though?"

"Nothing, really. What about you?"

"Nothing, just thinking about you. We should do something,"

"Do something like what?"

"I don't know; go to a movie, out to eat, or we could just chill at my crib,"

"I guess so. When?"

"If you don't have anything to do tonight..."

"I guess we can make something happen,"

"I'll pick you up, like nine, nine-thirty,"

"Okay,"

"I'll see you then, aight," I hung up the phone in amazement to myself like, *am I really about to go on a date?* My last date had to be at my senior prom so I wondered if I could remember how to do that.

Although, Joya lived maybe five minutes away, I arrived at her house around 9:45 that night, but ready to get things started. Rather than meeting her at the front door, I sat in the car and called her to come out to me. She hopped in with her face in awe at my ride.

"Nice car," she said excitedly.

"And you know this, baby," I replied when I hit the gas.

"Mm, what drugs do you sell?"

"Why does a man have to sell drugs to be successful?"

"A nice car does not equal success. Besides, this *looks* like the car of a drug dealer. If you don't sell dope, what do you do? Tell the truth," she confronted me. I hesitated. Honestly, I felt like Joya was way too smart to be messing around with me.

"I'm a salesman," I confessed.

"Dope sales," she snickered. "Just be honest about it; I didn't say anything about it. I just want to know the truth about what you do for a living,"

"Well, that's what I do; and I do it pretty well," I laughed.

"I bet. How many times you been arrested?"

"How do you know I've been arrested?"

"Because nobody's that good. Even the great Pablo Escobar has been arrested,"

"I've been arrested once, but that was a long time ago. How many times have *you* been arrested?"

"Zero, smartass. How old are you?"

"Twenty-four, you?"

"Twenty-three. Any kids?"

"Nope,"

"Me neither,"

"Do you want kids?" I continued. This became the longest conversation I ever had just getting to know somebody. In the past, there actually wasn't a whole lot I really wanted to know about a woman. I didn't care as long as they were down to get down. But Joya, she intrigued me. In the middle of Gina's Italian Restaurant, we sat and explored each other's minds. I didn't even know who I was anymore. I wanted to get in her jeans, but at the same time she was blowing me away with the way she expressed herself. Joya was beautiful, independent, and most importantly, she was real. She was the truth and the truth was her, even if it made her look bad. That was my kind of woman right there.

As the night came to a close, I thought I might push out a playa move and walk her to her door. I figured if I got that close to the front door, I could make my way inside the house, as well as other things. Joya took a step in and held me back with her hand on my chest.

"What do you think you're doing?" Joya questioned.

"What? I thought we could kick it a little bit. What, you thought I was gonna try to have sex with you. Aw, naw, I ain't even like that," I lied. I wanted some; I wanted some bad.

"Look, no offense, but I've been in this very situation many times before and maybe you're not like that, but I'm not willing to take that chance. So...bye," she responded, slamming the door in my face. That was rude as hell. Regardless of what

I really wanted, I still would've been cool with sitting up all night having a conversation with her.

   After arriving back home, I was tempted to call her just to tell her how messed up that was. She didn't have to leave me at the door like that. But then I thought I would just leave her alone for a while and forget the whole thing happened. By now, I needed to light a blunt.

2

As I lay back on the couch watching the gray smoke slowly emerge from my mouth in a graceful dance, I reminded myself the very reason I didn't fall in love; chicks are crazy. At first, Joya seemed like she had everything I was looking for, but she turned out to be like every other woman. Too bad since I was really feeling something for her.

Just when I was relaxing into a silent, purple haze, I felt a relentless vibration at my lower thigh. My cell phone startled me, but even more so when I saw Joya's name on the display. I scoffed at the thought of talking to her now and tossed the phone to the glass coffee table in front of me. Then, an even more forceful tremor bounced the phone around my table. I picked up this time.

"Hello," I answered.

"What are you doing?" Joya asked.

"At the crib, chilling,"

"If you're alone, can I come by?" she pleaded.

"I mean, I guess; if you want to,"

"What's your address?"

"I'm around the corner. Just come on Lewis; 32-44," I directed her. Her voice sounded as if her whole world had come crashing down on top of her ego and she needed a friend to talk to. I wasn't really her friend. But I *was* interested in what she had to say. Before long, I heard a knock on my door. Even though I was staring directly at her shadow through the sheer, burgundy curtains covering the open blinds, I sat for a second. It's not like I was in a hurry for something.

I didn't make her wait long, however. I turned the brass knob and pulled the door open, observing the remorse in her eyes. Joya stepped in nervously with a first attempt to make small talk.

"What's up?" she began.

"What's up?" I replied. I didn't know exactly what she

wanted from me.

"Wow, it's obvious you've been smoking on a little something,"

"I know you didn't come over here to tell me that,"

"No; I wanted to apologize. I shouldn't have slammed the door in your face like that,"

"It's cool," I lied; I was still hot about that.

"Truth is, I really do like you,"

"Yeah?" I smirked. My head fell slightly to the left and I tried hard to keep in the laughs that the burning bush let out. Meanwhile, Joya stared into my slanted eyes before squeezing both of my hands and placing them at the small of her back. She rested her hand on the back of my neck and guided my head towards her face, pressing her full lips against mine. With her tongue caressing my own, it was then I felt a tightening in my jeans. And just when I was about to go in for the score, she pulled away and rushed out of the house.

It was more than bizarre. Joya cast this spell that I almost wanted to be under. Less than five minutes ago I no longer wanted to pursue anything she had to offer; but now, it was like she unleashed a poison that made want to savor every part of her. And with that kiss, I became addicted.

Rumors spread when it came to be known that the dope boy and the ghetto snob had something going on together. Apparently, her friends thought she could do much better; and my friends, they too felt she was out of my league. But little did they know, I played the game well. I could always deal with what my boys said. After all, it's just talk. Joya, on the other hand, seemed to lose her mind. It bothered her when somebody disrespected people she cared about, and even more when they disrespected her.

I held her hand as I tried to calm her down. She was nearly hyperventilating, but with anger in her eyes. Joya proceeded to wear a groove through the brownish carpet of my bedroom floor, ranting hysterically. It was then, I couldn't take it anymore. I grabbed her waist in mid-stride and looked directly into her eyes.

"Baby," I began as she stilled. "Don't worry about them. It's just words. Not everybody will like the thought of us being together. Matter-fact, the whole city thinks you're better than me; so, if I'm straight, I know you should be." Joya breathed in one intense breath before dropping her shoulders abruptly, realizing my point.

"Why are you this smart?" she joked with a relieved smile. Wrapping her arms around my neck, she planted a light kiss to my jaw, then another on my blackening lips. As we shared in a few gentle kisses, I slightly nudged her body to fall back at the loose, charcoal bed cover. Her passion seeped through while I lied on top of her warming essence and felt the enthusiasm pass from her tongue to mine.

Joya pulled at my royal blue t-shirt and moved her hands from my oblique's to my sagging belt buckle. The pressure built up inside of me as I couldn't resist this fever. I snatched my shirt over my head, as she did the same. I forced her jeans from around her waist and watched her hips as they jumped from suffocation. Once my pants hit the floor, I fled to the wetness between her legs.

I moved vigorously with an excitement I could no longer contain. I was open and ready for whatever. Joya held tightly to my body, pressing her fingernails into my skin and whispering my name in my ear. She released one last passionate scream as I sank inside her. While some form of energy ran through my body, I rose from my position to grab my clothes and run to the bathroom to clean myself off.

I threw wintry water in my face, trying to keep my composure; I was breathless. My heart raced as I couldn't imagine her sweets tasting so good. Joya's body was my paradise island and I was destined to explore every inch. I could swear this girl had me hooked.

When I returned to the room, the lights were nearly dimmed to their lowest and Joya's body was outlined underneath the covers. For a second, I remembered that I never let chicks spend the night; especially after sex. But Joya lay so peacefully in her fetal position, and suddenly I didn't mind. I climbed on the bed beside her and watched her exhales until my own dreams appeared.

I awoke the next morning, somewhat drowsy but alert, to the sound of slamming drawers and cabinet doors in my kitchen. I changed quickly into a pair of gray sweatpants, leaving my chest bare, and met her there. She beautifully sported a North Carolina blue throwback jersey from my closet and the body-hugging jeans she wore the night before. She had pulled her hair back into a glossy ponytail that made a fountain just down her back. I sat at the round, oak table while she fumbled through my refrigerator; imagining her doing so every morning for the rest of our lives.

"Why do guys only buy junk food?" she started to herself.

"Because we don't have fine women to cook for us," I replied. Joya jumped from behind the refrigerator door, startled but then smiling as if she were happy to see me. She pranced over to me and greeted me with a kiss, and parking her behind on my lap.

"So, about this breakfast you want to cook for me," I continued.

"Well, I would but, one, you have no food, and two, I should go,"

"Go where?"

"To work,"

"What time you gotta be at work?"

"Ten; but I still have to go home and take a shower,"

"Can't you take a day off?" I pleaded, somewhat disappointed she was leaving.

"Nope, I have shit to do," she assured me, hopping from my knee. As she headed towards the front door, I stopped her.

"Hey!" I called. "Can I get my jersey back?"

"Later," she smiled.

Frankly, it turned me on how focused she was. Nothing made me happier than to have a woman I didn't *have* to take care of.

But I meanwhile battled to keep my mind off of the events from the night before, and what events could arise in the future. I was out of my element. It was more than uncommon for me to be completely consumed by a woman. My hustle, of course; my money, always; but never a woman.

Once I grabbed a bottle of water from the refrigerator and took a swig, I pulled myself back up the stairs and into a searing shower. Even there, my mind was set on Joya. No matter how hard I tried, I couldn't get her off my mind. And I really didn't want to. Staring into her face once I closed my eyes made me rethink my entire life. I didn't know what I was doing or where I was going. I wondered if I had more aspirations would I be better off. In some ways, I didn't know if I wanted to deal anymore. But if I stopped now, what would be next for me?

In the midst of trying to decide if my life had a future worthy of Joya's standards, I slipped on a black tank top, some solid black jeans, and a pair of black Timberland boots to prepare myself for a day of hustling. The first thing to do was to gather all of the work I planned on selling that day. I seemed to be running low with only three small baggies of weed and two bags of crack-cocaine just that same size. I didn't know if it was worth even stepping out of the house for that purpose. It would've been gone in two seconds and I only would've made parking meter money. I guess it was time to hit up my boy Derek for a connection run.

At the moment I slapped the lonely work on the kitchen table, there was a relentless banging at my front door. The knocking stunned me into a paranoid panic that the police had found me once again; and having the evidence lying out on the table was not about to help my case. I snatched the baggies from the table and fled to drop them in a place no one would think to look. When I was on my way to the second floor, one foot on the first step, I heard the anxious voice of Jordan.

"Aye, yo, Jay!" he yelled. My nerves came down a bit as I turned and drifted to the door. I twisted the knob to notice both Derek and Josh following behind.

"What's up; hey, Josh, where have you been? I think the last time I saw you was like two weeks ago, man," I started. Josh was a forlorn man in ways. Though he didn't get out much, he was a quiet player. The man stood six feet even with a strong demeanor like he was just waiting to punch somebody in the face. He had tattoos from the neck to the end of his arms, with his light skinned back completely covered. And I could swear that almost every time I saw him, he was brushing his low-cut fade. I guess chicks really dug pretty boys.

Meanwhile, the boys got comfortable on the couch while I sat in the corresponding chair adjacent to them, wondering to myself why they took it upon themselves to darken my doorstep; as if they had nothing better to do.

"Come on, man," Derek started with a devious grin. "Give up the 4-1-1; what happened to you all day yesterday? We know you were with that girl." Wiping my eyes, I sighed. I should've known this was why they came over.

"That ain't none of your business. Don't worry about what I do," I answered.

"Whatever, man," Derek continued, leaning forward. "Did you hit yet?"

"Once again, not your business,"

"That's a negative, as stuck up as she is." he heckled. The three of them laughed like they knew I would never hook up with Joya. Ignorant laughter.

"Ha ha, but you laugh real hard for some niggas who are completely wrong," I responded. They calmed down, eyes wide open, in disbelief.

"Word?" he said.

"That's right,"

"Was it good?"

"Immaculate; that's how good it was. A nigga had to pull out a fifty-dollar word for that one," I joked.

"Aye, what were you about to do, though?" Jordan asked.

"That reminds me, I was about to meet you at The Spot, but I have nothing so, Derek, I need you to hit up your connect real quick," I declared.

"I'm on it," Derek confirmed.

"While he's on that, yo, hook up the Madden," Josh interjected. While Derek did a quick run to the projects for a few bricks, I set up the Xbox for a few games of virtual football. There was nothing like a little football to take my mind off the grind. Aside from a little trash-talk, this was the only thing that seemed to keep me from getting into trouble as a kid. I was even quarterback on my varsity team in high school and almost went pro. That is, until I got arrested and the draft went to somebody else. Talk about devastation.

After Derek returned with a duffle bag full of work and witnessed me kill Josh on the game, we rounded up and got back on the job. The sun beat at us on the block with no mercy while we made that money and smoked our stresses away. The cool cash was enough to counteract a heatstroke. And as the amount added, I thought it was about that time to pay some bills before I would be on the street and in the heat for good.

Showing up to the house once my business was taken care of, I spotted a white Volkswagen Jetta parked directly in front. No others were ahead or behind, and I didn't see anyone who looked like they might have been waiting on someone. I took a deep breath and ignored the car, only to approach my front door in awe. It was already unlocked; but I checked the lock before I left.

I grasped the steel pistol at my waist as I entered the house slowly and on my toes. Leaving the door open, I crept in further and turned abruptly to point my gun at the unknown individual sitting on my sofa. When I pictured a woman's build, I moved in closer, lowering the gun, and realizing it was Joya. She sat with her legs crossed and a troubled look on her face. I had completely stopped in my tracks, still trying to figure out how she got into my house.

"Joya?" I began.

"Come here," she said.

"How'd you get in my house?"

"Sweetie, you leave a key in the mailbox. By the way, not so smart to do on this side of town,"

"Anyway, what's wrong?" I questioned, inching towards her and joining her on the couch. I leaned back with my eyes low as she watched me closely. As Joya moved near me, she scrunched her nose and pursed her lips, speculating, "Are you high?"

"A little bit," I laughed.

"That's not funny, Jayson," she continued as she shook her head in disappointment.

"That's exactly what I wanted to talk to you about,"

"What?" I wondered.

"The fact that all you do is smoke weed and sell drugs,"

"What about it?"

"I've been thinking. You're actually smart and you have the potential to get out of the SWATS and do something with your life, but you choose to stay here and waste your time,"

"Hold up, I thought you were cool with what I do. Now, all of a sudden, you wanna change me? I make money out here, so you either deal with it or you don't," I barked. She was beginning to irritate me. Joya was a beautiful woman who I wouldn't mind being with, but I could never sacrifice my survival technique just because she didn't like it.

"Look," she persisted. "I'm not trying to change you. I want you to be who you are, I'm just saying; when you're high, we're not on the same level,"

"Joy, I've been smoking since I was sixteen. Weed is the most harmless drug in the world, and I'm supposed to quit because you have a few reservations about it? I don't think so,"

"What grown-ass, black man in this neighborhood uses the word *reservations*?"

"And I'm high as hell right now, so why are you even mad?"

"Okay, true. But can we limit the habit to like a blunt a day?" she pleaded.

"What is this, a negotiation?" I asked sarcastically.

"You're not gonna make this easy for me, are you?" she responded. I was against this whole idea. My own mama didn't control me when it came to the weed I smoked and the drugs I sold; nor did she try to. If Joya had a problem with me, she could always walk out, even though I didn't want her to. I wondered if this was something she would actually leave over. Then I glanced over at her big eyes, begging me to agree with her.

"I just won't smoke around you," I decided. In a way, it appeared that Joya just wanted more for me than what I had; so I guess I could understand that. But then again, these women can be sneaky enough to get you aligned with their own blueprint of what your future should be. I just had to be careful.

My high was starting to come down when I thought this conversation was over. Somehow, Joya got on the subject of my goals as a kid; something I didn't really think about after I got locked up. When I thought about it, all I ever really wanted to do at that point was make money. And that's what I was doing. But she got more in depth, forcing me to think about specific career plans. I didn't feel too comfortable talking about my football days because I couldn't see myself getting back in the game, and that, honestly, hurt my heart so I just kept it to myself.

Joya kept pushing me to confront my past and I continued to lie like there was nothing that had my attention. I didn't know why it was so important to her; why couldn't she just let it go?

"You're telling me there was nothing you liked doing?" she pressed.

"Nope," I lied. She stared into my face as I kept quiet, focusing my eyes on the table in front of me.

"You're lying," she accused. "Tell me." My eyes jumped to hers and I couldn't keep it in any longer.

"Football," I confessed.

"Football? Really? Since when do you play football?"

"I don't. I *used* to play,"

"Why'd you quit?"

"Because nobody recruits seniors from jail,"

"So that's what happened? You gave up the only thing you ever loved because you got arrested? Let me guess; it was on a drug charge," she ranted.

"Why does it even matter?"

"Because," Joya snapped, raising both her voice and her body. "I cannot stand it when people give up so easily. The very thing that you let take your dream, you decide to do *that* for the rest of your life. I can't believe you gave up a chance to play college football, with a chance to go pro, all because you got arrested. That was so dumb,"

"Actually, I was about to be drafted straight to the pros to play for the Falcons," I told her. The fury filled her eyes and her jaw dropped in awe.

"Are you serious right now?! Jayson, if you were that good, man, try again," she suggested.

"Joya, you don't get it. After I got out, they had already replaced me and there was nothing I could do. I didn't even wanna keep playing after that. It was over," I admitted.

"It was only over because *you* said it was over. I can't believe you let that stop you,"

"What, am I supposed to try out again?"

"Uh, yeah! You're all of twenty-four, I think you have time before they call you a veteran. You know what, just think about it, okay. I gotta go," she said, stepping over my feet and angrily making her exit.

Sometimes, I hated when she, or any other woman for that matter, had a point. When the NFL rejected me, I was so emotional that I didn't know where else to go. I got so caught up with Derek's lifestyle that it became my own and I didn't care anymore. My head was going through the motions. To make matters worse, that moment was when I was starting to feel for Joya even more. No chick had ever cared so much about *my* life; as long as I was giving them what they needed, they were cool. So, where had she been all my life?

I sat on that thought for a few weeks while I tried to figure out if I was ready to get back on the field. Spending more and more time on the street corners, I couldn't help, though, but to throw that to the back of my mind. I knew exactly what I had in

Joya, but at the same time, I had this habit of checking out the competition. I was a slave to the Georgia peach that sat proudly on a woman's back; and every time one passed by me, I wanted to get a taste of the juices.

It was a major challenge to remind myself that I was already involved with somebody I actually liked. But one clear day struck a nerve in both me and Joya. The brisk wind blew through the parts of my braids and Joya's curled ponytail brushed against my arm as I held her hips on a walk through a strip mall. The image took me by surprise when my ex-girlfriend strut past us like a supermodel, only in Adidas instead of stilettos. Her oval eyes followed me as they grabbed hold of my neck and twisted it towards her.

Diamond was a beast. She was an attractive five-foot-six as a svelte woman with golden skin and a cute face. The crimped waves of her coal-colored hair allowed a slight breeze to flow along her silver, body-hugging dress, squeezing tight to her cleavage and letting loose at mid-thigh. For a second, she somewhat enticed me with the cherry lollipop she rolled around her mouth and kissed with her equally shining lips. I forgot Joya was even there until her voice overpowered my delusion.

"Seriously?" she uttered. My eyes shot back to her view as I noticed myself in flames looking into the darkness of her eyes.

"Babe, it's not what you think," I started.

"It's not what I think? I think you were staring, that's what I think. Or is it just my imagination?"

"Look, that was just an old girlfriend. She caught me by surprise, that's all,"

"If she's an old girlfriend, then why would you allow her to steal your attention like that?" she questioned. I was speechless. I couldn't tell her I had a weak moment and forgot how fine she was.

"I can't believe you," she scoffed. "I'm going home; don't follow me." Joya took off in the opposite direction as I called her back to me, hoping that I could explain myself and that she would listen; but she ignored me. I was pissed.

Diamond didn't say a word to me but still made the situation difficult. I swear I hated her. The last time I saw her was two months earlier when we broke up, after I learned that she did a little more than strip at Magic City. This chick not only gave it up to whoever slipped her a few dollars, but she was also playing mommy to three kids. I couldn't be bothered with that drama.

Meanwhile, I couldn't be bothered with Joya either. I gave her the space she wanted and decided to wait until she came to me. I guess she had a change of heart later that night because she asked to join me at Club 112 as I was on my way to meet with my boys. A part of me wanted to hit the club to get away from Joya but, in a way, I wanted to see her just to reassure myself that everything was cool between us. That's when I was starting to worry about myself and the affect she had on me.

In about ten minutes I was honking my horn outside of her house, waiting for her to make an appearance. She burst through the front door and hustled to my car with eagerness in her eyes. She didn't even try to hide the shape of her form, then again she never did. She breathed deeply under an ice blue, cut-off t-shirt with a royal blue butterfly drawn out in rhinestones. Her jeans were an even darker denim, and as tight as her shirt but around the waist. As she stepped her matching Lady Timberlands on the beige car rug, I noticed pale blue ribbons woven into the two French braids hanging over her shoulders.

Joya was surprisingly in a good mood considering how she'd lost her mind earlier. In fact, it was almost as if she had forgotten the tantrum she threw. I almost began to recap the situation with her to humor my confusion until I stopped myself to realize, if she can forgive and forget, then why interfere with that? I felt like I kept one eye on the road and one eye on her until arriving alongside the full street lined around Club 112.

We pushed past the eager crowd as I gripped Joya's hand tightly and moved through the humidity and drum-busting music. I spotted my boys posted in a booth in a corner deep into the room. I pulled Joya towards them and greeted each one with a ghetto handshake; a tight grasp and a yank to the floor. As I formally introduced Joya to Derek, Josh, Jordan, and Shawn, she gave them a head-nod before turning her head to scope out the rest of the place.

I was wrapped up in a conversation with Jordan when I noticed out the corner of my eye the way Derek's head was bent back and his lips pursed, staring intensely at Joya. I looked back at Joya and saw she shared the same expression. If I didn't know any better, I would say this wasn't the first time they had met. The blaze in her eyes told me that their last meeting was not a happy one.

"I'm sorry, have you met?" I asked, pointing back and forth at the both of them. Derek ignored me while Joya yelled into my ear how she was going to look for some friends and took off. I honestly didn't know what just happened. Of all people to have a past, it had to be my best friend and my girlfriend; something didn't sound right. I slid in next to Derek on the end and before I could ask him anything, Shawn interrupted.

"Man, I know you're not in love now," he snubbed.
"Man, ain't nobody in love. And even if I was, man, at least I got a girl," I snapped back. The banter was heavy and nearly serious. It felt good to finally partake in the sole reason we were gathered together that night; just to be boys. This battle of the dozens got hotter and more exciting; it was to the point I had forgotten Joya was even with me. However, then, her head belted in front of mine and she grabbed my arm, pulling me to the dance floor.

Taking our spot on the floor, a whole different side of Joya let loose. The bump and the grind at my crotch caught me by surprise. I held onto her waist with her every twist and turn as she grabbed my neck and practically made love to me in the middle of the room. At that moment, the dirty south was given a new name; and that name was Joya Jones.

Eventually, Joya grew tiresome and ran off to the bar for a little hydration. I thought I would join her right after I made a visit to the bathroom. As I started off, the thin hand of a woman slid up the front of my chest and stopped me in my tracks. At first, I thought Joya just couldn't stay away from me long. But I turned to lay eyes on a tall, glass of chocolate milk wrapped in a strawberry red, strapless number that cut just below her womanly essence. She shyly giggled as she moved a few strands of her auburn curls from her eyes. I jumped back, not really knowing what to do. The girl had a body to die for, but all I could do was see the fire in Joya's eyes, feel the burn of the bruises I would have on my body, and hear the ringing in my ears from the shrill screaming she would do as she cursed me out. I thought to myself, *nah, I'm good.* I shook my head at the girl and started to walk away when she skipped in front of me, pressing the tips of her fingers into my chest.

"I just want a dance; you can't dance with me?" she yelled in my ear, stepping up on the balls of her feet. I grabbed both of her hands and replied, "I'm good." I started to walk around her when I saw Joya in front of me, her face red like a ripe berry. She was holding a plastic cup of the same color when she took a sip and approach the tipsy woman at my feet.

"What the hell do you think you're doing?" Joya questioned, leaning into the girl's ear. She jumped and spun around as she saw Joya's lips pursed and her eyebrow raised. She smiled at Joya with a playful gaze when she responded, "Hey, Joya, girl; I didn't see you there." Joya snatched her arm and pulled her out to the dim parking lot outside of the club.

"What's your problem, Joy? You act like I want to fuck him," the girl started.

"That's because I know you would've tried, Nadia. How many times have I told you not to come on to random guys like that?" Joya replied. It didn't dawn on me how well she knew this girl.

"You ain't my mama! I'm grown, I can do what I want,"

"Can you? So you want to intentionally get pissy drunk and end up like you did the last time? Some life,"

"Look," I interrupted. "Since she's supposed to be your friend, let's just take her home,"

"No," Joya objected. "She's grown and she wants to act like a hooker, so she can't hitch a ride like one,"

"Oh, so I'm a hooker now?" Nadia said, stumbling closer to Joya. "That's exactly how you're acting right now. Look at you, you can't even stand up straight. This is why I can't take you anywhere when people are drinking because you feel that's a need to get toasted. I told your ass to go to rehab, but you didn't wanna listen. So, you know what, I'm done. I can't spend my life keeping you out of trouble. Jayson, let's go," Joya pleaded. She motioned for me to follow her as she stormed off in the opposite direction towards my car.

Joya never struck me to be the type to leave a friend to fend for themselves. However, she was the type to be unorthodox when it served a purpose. Either way, her mind was made up, so why worry about it? I didn't know that girl.

3

I woke up alone just before noon when an aroma, not unlike what I was used to growing up with my mother, crept through my bedroom door and up my nostrils. My mouth started to water as I made my way to the brightened kitchen and spotted a layout of home-cooked scrambled eggs, bacon, spicy sausage, and buttered biscuits. I was so hype that Joya cooked for me I didn't waste time dipping my fork into the steamy goodness. The first bite took me back to those good mornings I had as a child with just me, my mother, and my sister; back when things were simple. It forced me to crack a smile. I picked up my plate and went into the living room where Joya sat Indian style on the sofa as she watched television. I sat down next to her.

"So," she began smiling. "I see you found your breakfast."

"Mm hm. I didn't know you could cook." I replied.

"I'll take that to mean you like it. But hey, since you're up now I'm going to run home and take a shower and I'll be back in a little bit."

"Cool." I said as I nodded my head. Joya gave me a quick kiss on the cheek and scampered out the door. It was then that I took some time to think about Joya's qualities, not just as a woman, but as a person. I thought about how everybody else felt like she was too good for me. But I didn't think that was entirely true. In my opinion, Joya wasn't out of my league because she was made to be the only player on my team. The city of Atlanta thought they knew her, but they really didn't know her at all. Damn, I picked a good one this time.

I was so into my thoughts of Joya that I almost didn't hear my phone ringing. I noticed it was my mother calling. I hadn't been to see her in nearly a week and she was probably calling to find out why.

"Hey, Mama," I answered.

"So, word around town is that you have a new girlfriend," she started. My mama always did get right to the point.

"Wow, is it that serious? As big as this city is and everybody seems to know."

"Well, had you just told me from the beginning it *wouldn't* be that serious."

"I'm sorry, Mama. I didn't wanna tell you until I knew it was worth telling you about."

"Okay, I guess I understand that. So, what's she like? Please tell me she's not like that other girl you were with. What was her name? Jewel? Sapphire?"

"Diamond, Mama,"

"Right! Diamond. I knew it was some jewelry. She's not like her is she?"

"No, no. She's nothing like her. She has a good job, sophisticated. She even asked me about my football days. She wants me to get back into it,"

"Oh, yeah? You were so focused back then. Maybe you should start playing again. I remember how much you used to love that. You shouldn't have quit,"

"That's what she's saying,"

"Hm, I think I like her already. What's her name?"

"Joya,"

"Oh, that's pretty. How long have the two of you been together?"

"Just a little over a month,"

"And I'm just now finding out about her? That's deep,"

"I'm sorry, Mama,"

"Now, I know what goes on in the bedroom is none of my business but I just want to make sure that you remember that both of you should get tested. You know girls around here don't know their cooch from a hole in the wall,"

"Wow, Mama, okay."

"Seriously, Jayson. You need to talk to her about that,"

"I will," I complied. These were the times when I wished my mother wasn't so cool. I knew she was looking out for me like she knew how, I just preferred that she wasn't so blunt about it.

"So, are you still selling drugs?"

"Mama,"

"Okay, okay. Since you don't want to talk to me anymore, I'll let you go. I love you,"

"Love you too, Mama," I hung up. *So much for subtlety*, I thought. Though I giggled at the thought of my mother being so direct with me when it came to my sex life, I took it to heart at the same time. I gave it some serious consideration because no matter how much I tried to avoid it, the issue was alive and well. However, getting tested for sexually transmitted diseases is not exactly the easiest way to start a conversation. I wasn't worried that Joya would be offended. In fact, she would view it as me being a responsible grown man. But how do I say it? When do I say it? Man, I don't know.

As I finished my breakfast, I rose from the couch and made my way into the kitchen. Just when I sat my plate in the sink, *Pop! Pop! Pop! Pop!* The sound of screeching tires echoed outside of my windows. I ducked down for only a minute to make sure the coast was clear before getting up to peek out my window. Normally the street was packed full of people but at this particular moment, it was a ghost town. I couldn't see anything or anyone until I looked slightly to the left and noticed bright red. The color was wrapped around a female's body, which lied motionless in the middle of a dimly lit alley directly across from my front porch. I shook my head in shame, trying to resist the urge to walk outside and see who this unfortunate creature was. I wondered if anyone had called the police. Probably not since no one was really a fan of the cops. Someone should've at least called for an ambulance. I didn't want to get involved, though. Sooner or later, whoever she was would be found; squad cars patrolled my neighborhood on a regular basis.

It didn't take very long before police sirens rang throughout my neighborhood and settled across the street. I casually walked onto my porch and sat at the top step, looking on at the scene. It was chaos as they rolled out the yellow crime scene tape, blocking off the area and controlled the slowly forming crowd of bystanders. I wondered who she was, what she did or what she didn't do. Who thought it was that necessary to take this girl's life? Maybe she had just been in the wrong place at the wrong time or had gotten mixed up with the wrong people. I pulled at the side of my gray sweatpants in contemplation. Just as a daydream started to set in, Derek ran up to me, pulling me out of it.

"Hey, what's up, Jay?" he greeted me as I rose from my seat.

"What's going on, fam?" I replied.

"Nothing much. You know what happened over here, right?"

"Not too much," I said, rubbing my goatee. "All I know is that some chick got shot,"

"Do you remember that girl that you left the club with last night?"

"Joya?" I asked. What did Joya have to do with this? I knew that wasn't her on the pavement since she had just left my side less than an hour ago.

"Not her, the other girl," he said, referring to Nadia.

"Oh, yeah. What about her?"

"That's who that is over there," Derek was pointing at the corpse being lifted into the ambulance. I couldn't believe it. I thought that dress looked familiar but it was too hard to tell without being any closer. Joya would be devastated the moment she heard and because it happened here, in front of my home, it became my responsibility to tell her.

"Are you serious?" I continued in awe. Derek just nodded his head. "Are you sure that's her? How do you know?"

"I can't get into all that. What you need to worry about is how you're gonna tell your girl,"

"Aight, man. Let me go do that now and I'll catch you later,"

"Cool," he said as he gave me a gentle pat on the arm and ran off in the direction he'd come. I took a deep breath back into the house and grabbed my phone. This would not be easy. It never was. I've had to tell too many people about the death of their family and friends, and frankly I was sick of it. But either way, it had to be done. I dialed her number slowly. With every ring I felt more and more pressure build in my stomach. Then I heard her voice; so ignorant to everything that was going on that it sounded sweet and innocent.

"Hey, babe. What's going on?" she answered.

"Joya, there's something that I need to tell you," I said. My voice leaked sadness and concern.

"Okay...what?"

"Nadia got shot," I blurted. Joya fell silent. I didn't want to speak until she had time to process what I was saying.

"What? Um...are you sure? How do you know? When did this happen?"

"It happened just today. She got shot across the street from my house,"

"Do you know if she's okay?" she asked as she struggled to get her words out. I could tell that she was fighting back tears but was losing the battle.

"Sweetie, they took her away in a body bag. She's gone," I said. Through her continuous sniffing, I convinced her to stay in the house and I would be over as soon as I took a quick shower. I couldn't wait to feel that hot water hit my back with so much force that it nearly stung. I let the shower massage my muscles and the steam open my senses as much as possible before I had to comfort Joya. Putting on a pair of black jeans and a gray tank top, I just shook my head. What a motherfucking morning.

Joya opened the door with red eyes and a wet face. She looked as though she'd been crying for days. I didn't say anything before tightly wrapping my arms around her. I kissed her forehead as I led her to the couch. Joya seemed adamant in believing that Nadia's death was her fault. She felt that, if she hadn't left Nadia alone the previous night, she wouldn't have been killed. But it was my job to convince her otherwise. I couldn't remember ever having to do this with any of my previous relationships. I guess that's one thing that told me how Joya was different. Although it was an unfortunate situation, Joya and I were sharing a moment that said a lot about what she meant to me.

When she finally stopped crying, Joya stared directly into

my eyes.

"Could you go?" she asked. *I'm sorry, what?*, I thought. I took time out of my day to make sure she was alright and she's kicking me out? What part of the game was this?

"What?" I questioned.

"No, it's not that I don't appreciate you being here for me, I really do, I just...I need to be alone right now. I need to get my mind together,"

"Are you sure you don't want me to stay?" I wondered in confusion.

"Yeah, I'm sure. For real, thank you for telling me and for being here. It means a lot." she said. I kissed her damp lips and headed out the door. The stiff breeze blew relentlessly in my face as I walked around the corner, still in a puzzled mind frame. I couldn't understand where her head was. What had I done to make her feel like she didn't want to be around me? But I couldn't stay stressed about it. I had money to make and this little incident slowed down my grind.

I was short on weight. In my nightstand I only had two bags of weed, no crack rocks, and only a few bombs of cocaine. I could've sworn I had way more than that stashed away. I called Derek at the spot and told him I needed some work ASAP. I gave him an hour but within twenty minutes, he and the rest of the boys were knocking at my door with black duffle bags in each hand full of more than enough product. Each man walked proudly into my kitchen as they dropped the bags on the table, counter, and floor; all except for Kris, who had just gotten out of jail only a couple of weeks earlier.

Standing at just five feet tall, Kris was not your ordinary cat. He may have been overcompensating for his lack of height because with his stocky build, he played the tough guy role like he couldn't be touched or tamed. The man has thought himself to be unstoppable after doing ten years in prison for what he claimed was involuntary manslaughter. But everybody that knew him was clear that the man was dead on purpose. Either way, between his short fuse and his prison record, he came with a lot of drama but was the man to go to when you needed him. That's why we kept him around.

I took a blunt from my pocket and lit it in silence before shuffling through the merchandise. Bricks on top of bricks on top of bricks filled my kitchen. Everything I had asked for was right in front of my face putting money-green dollar signs in my eyes. I was back on top and it sure felt nice.

"Say, man," Kris started. "What happened across the street?"

"Girl got shot," I answered. I let out the thick smoke I held in my lungs.

"For real? Do you know who?"

"Chick named Nadia,"

"Oh, were you cool with her?"

"Not really. She was a friend of my girl," I continued. I inhaled deeply and let the power of the grass take over my mind. I was flying high on a magic cloud, so relaxed that I felt damn near loopy. Shit, come down for what? My eyelids were beginning to drop when there was a heavy knock on my front door. I sighed as I slowly made my way to the door. I put one hand on the knob and yelled, "Who is it?"

"Atlanta PD. We need to ask you some questions about a homicide that happened over here today," the man said. I cursed to myself while my boys rushed to move the duffle bags into my bedroom. I ran to get an ashtray to put out my blunt before shoving it in my pocket.

"I don't know what happened," I yelled through the door.

"Sir, please open the door. We just want to ask a few questions, that's it," he said. I took a deep breath and pulled the door open a few inches. I looked out at two fair-skinned officers, one appearing to be at least twenty years younger than the other, both jumping back at the stench emanating from my house. They placed their hands to their noses before asking if they could come in. I immediately declined.

"Why do you need to do that? You said you wanted to ask questions. You can ask me from here," I told him. My eyes still hung low and my words sounded almost lazy. They peered at me suspiciously.

"Sir, have you been smoking marijuana?" he asked. Dumb question.

"Why would you ask that?" I replied nonchalantly. By now, a grin was appearing on my face.

"We can smell marijuana all the way out here,"

"Incense," I lied, shrugging my shoulders. The two of them looked at one another in disbelief before asking me to step outside. Once I was on the porch, my boys were asked to join me as the younger officer called for backup and stepped through the door into my house. I prayed that the drugs were hidden well enough, not to mention the guns I kept around the house. I nervously waited. I couldn't stop fidgeting, rubbing my face, and scratching my head. I had enough weight to do some serious time. In some cases, it was ten years for every bullet, so if I got caught, my life was done.

"Why are you so nervous, son?" the balding officer asked.

"Man, don't you have to ask my permission to search my house? This doesn't seem right," I questioned.

"Well, if you didn't do anything, you don't have anything to worry about." he said.

"I'm just saying..." I continued. The other officer appeared again with a dubious look upon his face and shaking his head. I felt as though he was about to tell me something that I didn't want to hear. He whispered something to his buddy who ran to his squad car and came back quickly. Before I could say *amen* I was being handcuffed.

"Who owns this house?" he asked.

"Man, I do," I answered.

"Alright, you are being charged with possession of illegal narcotics with intent to distribute, as well as seven counts of possession of a deadly weapon. And you are now also a suspect in the homicide of Nadia Shepherd. You have the right to remain silent..." he began. I thought to myself, *you have got to be shitting me*. I couldn't believe it. Not again. The last time I got arrested I swore to myself that I wouldn't let it happen again.

I was too smart for that. And my boys just stood there and watched me get put in the back of a police car and hauled off to jail. *Son of a bitch!*

Anger just flooded my veins. The more they questioned me about Nadia, the worse my mood became. They stared me dead in the face and spoke to me as if I had actually done it. But why would I murder someone in front of my own house? That's just stupid. I thought about Joya. I was really beginning to catch feelings for her and I didn't want to lose her to this life. I was facing too much time and I knew she wouldn't wait for me. There's no way she cared that much.

First chance I got I called Derek to come bail me out. Apparently he had already been trying to get me out but not only did they keep my bond amount a secret, they also tried to make him a suspect in Nadia's case as well. At that point, he was too scared to do anything. I told him to call Joya and tell her what was going on. Whatever my bail was, he would give her the money to get me out. This was not the place for me.

While sitting in a cold cell in holding, I did something I hadn't done in a long time; I prayed. I didn't know if God would even want to listen to somebody like me but I had to be in the back of His mind somewhere if Joya had come into my life. I swore I would change my whole life if He would get me out of there. I would do anything to keep myself out of prison. I was alone with my thoughts for what felt like an eternity, and I was becoming anxious. Suddenly, my cell door was unlocked as the sound of the latches echoed the hallway. A box-shaped guard led me to a large room with several other inmates looking at their loved ones through plate glass. In a bright orange jumpsuit, I walked to my seat and laid eyes on Joya.

I had never been so happy to see the face of a woman who wasn't my mother or my sister. Her bright eyes were piercing my soul as I picked up the phone and waited to hear her voice. I was good as long as she didn't look me in my face and tell me she was leaving me.

"Did Derek tell you everything?" I asked her.

"Yeah, he told me," she responded nonchalantly. It sounded almost as if she didn't care.

"And you know they're trying to blame me for what happened to Nadia?"

"Yeah, he told me that too. Now, let me get this straight. You had drugs *and* guns on you?"

"They weren't on me. That bullshit cop thought I was high and, next thing I know, he's searching my house,"

"Were you high?"

"That's not the point. The point is I'm facing like fifteen years on some fucked up charges,"

"Okay," Joya paused. She rubbed her forehead in frustration. "You said they searched your house. Did they have a warrant?"

"No,"

"Did they ask you?"

"No. All they said is, *"We smell weed so come outside"*,"

"Well, they might try to use probable cause but if they didn't even ask you, if they just walked in without a warrant, nothing they found can be used in court. Are the guns even registered?" she said. I looked at Joya with my head slightly cocked because she knew damn well they weren't.

"Stupid question," she said underneath her breath. "Look, either way, we can spin this to work in your favor. But there's no guarantee that it'll definitely work,"

"How do you know all this?"

"That's the benefits of working at a law firm. I'm only a legal secretary but I might as well be a lawyer," she smiled.

"Good to know. Did Derek give you my bail money?"

"I've got your back. Just wait here, it shouldn't be long," she answered. Hers face became somewhat somber while she forced a smile and got up to leave. Ten minutes, or two hours later because I couldn't tell the difference, and I was finally let go. I sauntered down the steps of the precinct as the warm sun kissed my skin and I thanked God to myself. I noticed Joya leaning against her car with her arms crossed. She was looking away through her large Dolce & Gabbana sunglasses as she stood in a

31

pink tank top and black short shorts. Her hair blew across her face when she saw me. As I approached her, I hugged her tightly when she said into my ear, "You owe me."

Come to find out, my bond was five thousand dollars. Normally, a man of my status didn't care, but business had been a little slow lately so it put a major dent in my finances.

"Mm hm," Joya continued. "That was my moving money too; you're lucky I love you,"

"Wait a minute, what?" I paused. I wasn't sure what had just happened. What was Joya talking about when she said that it was her moving money? And how is that her money when it came from me? I know she didn't expect me to fund her trip to who knows where without even discussing it with me. Where does that leave us? And now she was proclaiming her love for me for the first time? My mind was a cyclone. I just blurted out the first thing that came to mind.

"You're moving? Where? When?" I said. Joya let out a sigh.

"Oh, don't worry about that right now. We can talk about it later." she dismissed. I fell silent. The whole ride back to my house had me thinking about this one statement Joya had made. It bothered me so much that, even though I wanted to say something to her, I couldn't figure out where to start. The moment we pulled up in front of my house, Joya attempted to get out the car when I stopped her.

"Joya," I began. "Did you mean it when you said you love me?"

"Yes. I wouldn't say it if I didn't mean it," she said.

"Well, if you love me then why are you planning to leave me?" Joya's face went from peaceful to vexed.

"What are you talking about?" she asked.

"Well, for starters, *moving* money? Are you planning a permanent vacation any time soon?"

"Baby, that was before I met you. I was planning on moving to New York but then you came along so I've been re-thinking the whole thing. I was going to tell you when I was sure,"

"Yeah, okay. I'll give you that. But why did you say the

money was yours? I told Derek to give you the bail money. Are you trying to tell me he didn't do it?"

"I can honestly say he didn't give me the money,"

"Why didn't you just say that? I'll just talk to him and figure out what happened,"

"No. It's fine. Not a problem,"

"No, that's supposed to be my boy and he didn't do what I asked. I need to figure out why," I retorted before leaving the car. Something was not right about this. I could buy that Joya planned on moving before she met me, but what I couldn't swallow was why Derek never gave her the money for my bail. It wasn't a matter of him being unable to get the money because it was all cash hidden in the wall of my bedroom closet and the nigga had a key to my house. Maybe he didn't trust her with it. Maybe he thought she would take the money and run. All I knew was that someone was keeping a secret and I just had to find out who it was.

4

I was in the process of looking for a new job and was about to hop in my car when I saw my boys coming down the street. I greeted them one by one but I really wanted to have a discussion with Derek. I had been holding off this conversation until the right time presented itself, but a month had gone by and I couldn't procrastinate any longer. I pulled him to the side, cutting to the chase.

"Why didn't you give that money to Joya like I asked you to?" I started.

"Man..."

"That five-grand came out of her pocket. That's not how it was supposed to go,"

"How did that bitch get five-grand?"

"Yo, man, the name-calling has got to stop,"

"Look, Jay, you're my boy. You're practically my brother. Trust me when I say you don't want to mess with that girl. She's got your nose wide open and you act like you're all in love. Cut that out. It's not gonna last,"

"Bro, don't disrespect my relationship. Joya is a hell of a lot better than these other whores out here. That's for damn sure,"

"So, now it's a relationship?"

"Don't act brand new. Point being, she's not going anywhere. So deal with it," I said. Derek was getting on my last nerves when it came to Joya. He acted as though she was the worst woman in the world. I still didn't know how they'd known each other. And personally, I didn't really care. This dislike for one another had to end.

I turned to walk away from Derek and just when I lit a blunt from my pocket, I heard the hard pounding of a high-heel shoe on the pavement. I slowly raised my head and looked to my left as this vixen stopped traffic with her seductive face and hourglass body. As the sun danced across her skin-tight red t-shirt and blue skinny jeans, she approached me as if she was on a mission. I stared at her in disgust.

"Hi, Jayson," she grinned.

"What the fuck do you want?" I asked. Why beat around the bush?

"Is that how you greet the girl you almost married?"

"Almost what?" I nearly choked. "I was only with you for a couple of weeks and that was what *you* wanted. Why in the hell would I marry you when you fucked every nigga in the hood, not to mention my own cousin? Take your trifling ass on somewhere, nasty ho," I barked.

"You know what? Fuck you, nigga! Don't nobody want you. You know you miss all this!" she screamed. Before I could respond, Diamond stomped off in the opposite direction when she threw her middle finger in the air. I couldn't care less about how angry Diamond may have been. If you asked me, the angrier she was the better. Maybe then she'd realize how much I couldn't stand her and leave me alone for good.

Diamond brought back so many embarrassing memories for me. I could never figure out how her promiscuity got past me. She was literally the town whore and everybody knew it, except for me. Paying her for sex only made it more satisfying. In fact, that's how she lived outside of stripping at Magic City. Only when I caught her sucking my cousin's dick did I find out her story. To my surprise, she had three kids that had been taken away from her, which is something she never mentioned. If you asked her, she never had any kids. She showed herself as living proof that you can't turn a ho into a housewife. And after her, I vowed I would never get into another relationship; until two months later I was drawn to Joya, who had more than just an effect on me.

Being around Diamond made me miss Joya's face even more than I already had. I called her a few times but got no answer. For a while, I let it roll off my back and went back to my hustle on the block until nightfall. At that point, I was beginning to get worried. I hadn't heard from her all day. Not a phone call, not a text message. Nothing. As soon as I wrapped things up at the spot I rushed over to her house. Her car was still parked outside but, when I knocked at the door, there was no answer. My polite knocking turned into a banging with the side of my fist while I rang the doorbell repeatedly and screamed her name. Finally Joya snatched open the door.

Her face was puffy while her hair was in a messy ponytail. She wore a white tank top and underwear under a long bathrobe. It was like she was the poster child for depression. I figured she was still dealing with Nadia's death. However, a month had now passed and she hadn't shown any sadness since the funeral. I didn't know what was going on.

"Joya, what's going on? I've been trying to call you," I started. She motioned for me to come in as I followed her to her bedroom. She sniffed and rubbed her eyes as she got back into bed, lying in the fetal position underneath the wrinkled sheets. I kicked off my shoes and moved my body over hers before kissing her cheek and asking again, "What's wrong?"

"It's just..." she hesitated. "It's just that I found out that I'm pregnant,"

"Whoa, okay. So why are you crying?" I wondered. You'd think that someone like Joya would be happy to have a baby. Although in the back of my mind I wasn't too thrilled about it myself. Even though I cared about Joya, what we had was too new to bring a baby into the whole thing. I might have to start dealing again.

"Because this wasn't supposed to happen yet," she continued.

"So what are you gonna do?"

"What do you mean, what am *I* gonna do? We need to figure this out together,"

"Okay, so let's figure it out. Are you keeping it?"

"I don't know. With you not working, I can barely afford to pay my own bills. And it didn't help the situation having to bail your ass out of jail for five thousand dollars. I don't know what to do,"

"Well, we'll figure it out. It'll be cool,"

"Not necessarily. What if you get locked up, huh? You said it yourself; you might get like fifteen years. I can't have my baby growing up without a father," she said sadly. I hated that Joya was right. I tried to convince her that it would work out but I wasn't sure I even believed that. How could we raise a child together when the mother was struggling on her own and the father was in jail? Hm, déjà vu all over again. To add insult to injury, Joya and I were still in the process of getting to know each other. This pregnancy was a surefire way to create some tension that the two of us would not be able to handle together.

I took a deep breath and rose from the bed. Without saying a word, I hustled to the bathroom where I turned on the faucet and watched water fill the bathtub. I emptied a few capfuls of lavender bubble bath into the water until the foam reached the top. I rejoined Joya in her bedroom when I pulled her to her feet and led her to the bathroom. I removed the robe from her shoulders and slowly pulled off the rest of her clothes. She grinned as her face turned red and she stepped into the steamy bath.

I ran a soapy loofa sponge across her body without saying a word. As I moved down the length of her leg, I grabbed hold of her foot and began to massage it. Joya bit her bottom lip as she closed her eyes and lay back to enjoy herself. By the time I had finished the other foot, Joya leaned forward and held my face. As she kissed my lips, she thanked me for giving her what she needed. In some ways I surprised myself. I didn't know I had it in me to be so smooth. But then again, I always had a trick up my sleeve.

Once I got Joya out of the tub, I put her in my car. I needed to take her somewhere that would remind her of how things wouldn't be so bad if she and I were to have the baby. When she asked me where we were going, I just drove. The last thing I needed was for her to try and talk me out of it. This very place gave me a solution to any and all of my problems; never failed. I knew that this would get Joy's mind right without question.

We pulled into a quiet neighborhood, in front of a small brick house with a plastic patio chair sitting at the right-hand corner of the porch. The nighttime breeze stimulated my warm skin as it dried the sweat beads planted on my forehead. I grabbed her hand and led her to the door when I started to put the key in the lock.

"Is this your second home or something?" Joya asked. I laughed at the thought but continued my way into the house. We stepped into a neatly furnished living room where pictures of my sister and I covered the coffee table. Passing a picture on the wall of me in my high school football uniform, I led Joya through the conjoining dining room and into the kitchen.

"Hey, Mama," I said when Joya squeezed my hand tighter. I hugged my mother closely and gave her a gentle kiss on the cheek when I introduced her to Joya, who was smiling nervously. Her face lit up as she stared at me. My mother was a beautiful ebony woman who, although she was twice my age, never looked a day over thirty. Without my sister around, she became my best friend. At one point she was even my workout buddy until she got lazy one Saturday. She kept saying she would go back to the gym the following week but never did. But with ten extra pounds, she still looked good.

That night, Mama greeted us in a blue tank top and black sweatpants. Her hair was in rollers with a scarf wrapped around her head. Joya and I had taken a seat on the crème sofa and stared into my mother's face as she sat in the neighboring chair. Joya attached herself to me, holding on to my hand with full force. I knew she wasn't ready for this conversation but it was about that time for it to happen. This would be interesting.

"So," Mama started. "This is Miss Joya. She *is* gorgeous. I know the baby will be too,"

My jaw dropped slightly and Joya's head jerked quickly in my direction. How could she had possibly known that when I had just found out myself?

"Whoa," I said in shock. "How'd you know she's pregnant?"

"I didn't. I was just joking, but that doesn't mean I'm not happy for you. How far along are you, Joya?"

"Not very," she answered. "About six weeks,"

"Oh, okay." she smiled. Suddenly, the smile on her face turned down and she looked at me seriously. "You got into some trouble didn't you?"

"Damn, Mama,"

"Don't lie. I can see it in your face. How long?"

"I don't know yet. My court date won't be until next week,"

"What did they get you for? Possession?"

"Yeah,"

"I told you. Didn't I tell you to stop selling drugs? How much did they find on you, Jayson?"

"A lot,"

"How much is a lot?"

"A *whole* lot," I said. My mother let out a disappointed sigh when I continued, hoping to change her perspective. "But see, Joya was telling me that they can't use anything they found because they didn't have a warrant to search the house,"

"Really? Is that true?" she looked at Joya.

"Mm hm," Joya nodded. "I mean, they still might use probable cause but their evidence become inadmissible without a warrant,"

"And how do you know that? Are you in law school?"

"No. I work at a law firm so I learn a lot through the cases I help with,"

"Doing what? Paralegal?"

"Legal secretary,"

"Oh, well look at you," Mama smiled. I could see how impressed she was by the look in her eyes. She spoke to Joya like she was the ideal daughter and the perfect wife for me. Go figure. Then she brought up the baby again.
"So, do you want to keep it?" Mama asked, changing the subject.

"Well, at first I wasn't sure. I really didn't want to have to raise the baby if Jayson was in jail. I want it to have a father. But at the same time, I still want to have it," she confessed. Joya was now calm at the thought of having this baby. I knew that having a conversation with my mother would give her the reassurance she needed. Mama told me that if I couldn't beat my case,

I needed to do what I could for the baby from the inside. Easier said than done.

On the way home, I took the time to think about whether or not I really wanted this child. A part of me wasn't ready to be a father. But the rest of me couldn't wait to give someone else what I never had. With a case pending, I still wasn't working so my financial cushion could only last so long. If I went to prison, I planned to give the entire thirty thousand to Joya so she wouldn't have to struggle. I just wanted to be there for my kid, though.

I was lost in my thoughts and hadn't said a word to Joya the whole ride. Then she snapped me out of my haze.

"Hey," she said.

"What's up?" I replied.

"You never told me you had a sister,"

"Well, she's in jail. I don't like to talk about it that much,"

"So, in other words, the two of you were close and it was like losing your best friend,"

"Something like that," I told her.

My sister Traycee is just two years younger than me but always got into so much more trouble. She was remarkably beautiful for a girl her age with her flawless brown skin, long dark hair, and hourglass figure. Because she never really found her way in life, she hung around the one group of people who made her feel good about herself, older men. I tried to talk sense into her when I noticed them taking advantage of her, but my words fell on deaf ears. Tension only rose between the two of us and I didn't want to have any more complications at home.

It wasn't until four years ago, just after her eighteenth birthday, when the shit hit the fan. She had begun secretly dating a 28-year-old man who had recently moved to Atlanta. I had never heard of him but I was determined to find out who he was and what he was doing with my sister. The man was like a ghost, however. Even with all my connections in this town, I couldn't figure out anything about him. When Traycee had finally come to me about him, the only thing she said was that he put his hands on her and tried to rape her. That's all I needed to know. He would be dead by sundown. But before I could find out where he stayed, Traycee told me that she had already shot him. At that very moment I was angry that she hadn't come to me beforehand. If she had, she wouldn't be serving twenty-six years in prison right now. Traycee always was a free spirit. But that's my sister and I love her.

5

Wednesday had arrived, which meant my court date had arrived. The heat made it damn near impossible to keep my appearance presentable. I tried not to sweat through my pale blue collard dress shirt. I still walked with dignity up the courthouse steps with a navy tie around my neck, black slacks and wingtip shoes. Joya had done my braids the night before to make sure they were fresh but the sun beat down relentlessly on them. Though my chin was to the sky, stepping into the courtroom with Joya on my arm was one of the scariest things I had to do in my life. I just knew I wouldn't be leaving as a free man. As I noticed my mother sitting next to Derek and Shawn, I said a silent prayer to myself and waited for the trial to begin. I stood next to my female lawyer as the judge appeared. I focused on his round face as he spoke and asked me how I pled. *Not guilty.* Sweat dripped from his white hair as he explained the contents of the case through his thick southern accent. I kept my mind focused on what Joya told me. When he finally stopped talking, I interrupted before my lawyer could start with her opening statement.

"Your honor, may I say something?" I began. My lawyer, whom I had only met the day before, looked over at me as if speaking was not something I was allowed to do. But I had to mention this one way or the other. The judge nodded his head at me in approval so I continued.

"It's come to my attention that, because there was no warrant issued, all the evidence against me in this case is inadmissible,"

"Yes, that is true. But because this is not your first offense with a similar charge, you obviously haven't learned from your past mistakes,"

"I disagree, your honor. I'm under new direction, actively seeking an honest job. I am very capable of turning my life around," I said. At this point, I was winging it. I forgot I even had a lawyer. I said whatever I thought the judge wanted to hear. After all, it wasn't exactly a lie.

"What exactly is your *new direction*, Mr. Adams?" he asked.

"Well, actually she—"

"*She*? Well, is this lucky young lady here to vouch for your character?"

"Yes, I am, your honor," Joya interjected as she stood. She lit up the room in a brightly colored, spaghetti-strapped sundress with her hair pulled back in a sophisticated ponytail. She proudly stood beside me when the judge began to show a grin.

"Why, Ms. Jones, it's nice to see you again. But who are you to the defendant?" he said. I was taken by surprise. How did Joya know this man? She said that she'd never been arrested before, but was she lying? The curiosity was killing me.

"It's good to see you too, Jack. Well, I'm his girlfriend, and I can assure you that drugs are *not* a priority in his life and he has been looking for a job. You can trust that he is motivated to make a change," Joya argued.

"It also says here that you are a suspect in the homicide of Nadia Shepherd,"

"Your honor," my lawyer chimed in for the first time. "All of the firearms allegedly found at my client's residence have been processed and none have been linked to the crime scene,"

He paused and contemplated what he would do. A thousand things were running through my mind. The whole situation was surreal. From the look on his face, there was a chance that I would actually walk away from this. I held my breath.

"Well, for the first time in twenty-five years there is no deliberation involved in a case like this. Mr. Adams, you are extremely lucky that you know Ms. Jones. I'm letting you go; however, you will be on probation for twelve months. If you violate that probation in any way, there's at least a fifteen-year sentence behind it. And I guarantee you won't be able to talk your way out of that one," he informed, banging his gavel. I immediately let out a sigh of relief. For the first time, I was happy to be wrong, and my excitement was unmatched.

Joya was the most remarkable woman I had ever known. Had she really helped me talk my way out of a fifteen-year sentence? I couldn't believe it. When I asked her how she knew the judge she told me that she had assisted a lot of attorneys in the past with their cases; half of which were in his courtroom. It was then that I fell in love with her and I couldn't see my life without her. I held my girl close before stepping foot outside the courtroom. I kissed her, reminding her of how grateful I was to have her. Though she humbled herself, I knew how much it meant to her as well.

Damn, I needed a drink. All I wanted was about two blunts and a fifth of E&J Brandy. This was definitely a day to celebrate. We had just returned to my home from a celebration dinner at Red Lobster. I had invited Josh and Jordan to tag along because I needed all of my closest boys with me for this occasion. I sat comfortably on my sofa next to Joya when, to my surprise, Derek dropped down next to her. He placed a blunt between his lips when she nudged him in the arm.

"Please don't smoke that around me," she demanded.

"What? You don't smoke weed now?" Derek replied.

"I'm pregnant, you dummy,"

"Whoa," Derek paused. I had yet to tell any of my friends the news, not even Derek. But I pretended as though it was no secret. Everyone else whistled their congratulations. But Derek's face went blank. It was almost as if his face expressed some kind of betrayal against him. Something was definitely wrong. There had to be more to his feelings about Joya than he led on. Suddenly, Derek whispered something in Joya's ear causing her to lose her cool.

"Really, Derek? Really? That is so disrespectful." she said as if she was annoyed. Joya rose from the couch and stomped out of the room. It was clear to me that she and Derek had a connection that dated back longer than I could imagine, and I was becoming tiresome when it came to keeping the peace between them. It irked me. I asked everyone to leave while I spoke to Derek.

"Yo, Dee, how long have we been boys?" I asked, now standing by the front door with Derek.

"Forever and a day, why?" he replied.

"I've been getting this vibe between you and Joya. What's up with y'all?"

"Nothing, man," he scoffed.

"Doesn't seem like nothing?" I crossed my arms in suspicion. "Tell me the truth, man. Did y'all know each other before I hooked up with her?" Derek paused before he answered. He planted an embarrassed smile on his face as if he started to lie but knew I wouldn't buy it.

"Aight, man. Look, I met your girl down in Miami," he said.

"Miami?"

"Yeah. Remember when I went down there a couple years back to hook up with a friend of mine? Well, while I was down there at a little party one night, I saw your girl on the corner and got with her."

"Whoa. Got with her?" I repeated. I couldn't believe my ears. Fury rose from the pit of my stomach and for the first time I wanted to pound my fists into Derek's face. He did not just tell me he had sex with Joya. Not *my* Joya. Not the Joya that's about to have my baby. He must be mistaken. It had to be another girl that just looked like Joya. It didn't sound right. And Derek just stood there with a smirk on his face like she was just some ho around the corner.

"Man, why do you think I kept telling you not to mess with her? She's a ho," he continued.

"Man, if you fucked her why didn't you tell me before I got with her?"

"Because I thought you would've figured it out by now. She never mentioned she used to be a hooker?" he said. *Hooker?* There was no way that Joya was a hooker. She just didn't have that characteristic. Usually, you can tell a prostitute just by the sway in her step; kind of like Diamond. I didn't want to believe it. I felt betrayed and weightless like someone had just cut my legs off from under me. How was I supposed to look at her with the same kind of love I had just earlier that day in court? My head was pounding with confusion. I just stared at Derek. He continued to speak but I couldn't hear anything past *hooker*.

His lips were still moving but I pushed past him and ran up to my bedroom. I rushed into the dimly lit room where Joya was curled into the fetal position on top of the bed sheets fast asleep. I clapped my hands and yelled for her to get up before nudging her with the back of my hand. She slowly turned on her back as she awoke, groggy and stretching. Although she appeared vexed, I repeated for her to get up and pulled Derek into the room. Somebody, somehow, was going to tell me the truth. It was about time we clear the air.

"Tell me you didn't fuck him!" I started immediately as I pointed in Derek's direction behind me but kept my eyes focused on Joya.

"What?! Is that what he told you?" Joya replied.

"You might as well admit it. I told him everything," Derek interjected. Joya started past me clenching her teeth and charging at Derek. I grabbed her before her reach met his face and pushed her back. It must've been true. She was way too angry.

"That's some bullshit!" she screamed.

"Yes or no, Joya. That's all I need,"

"No,"

"Ooh, she's lying," Derek smiled.

"Shut up," she cried.

"I take that as a yes then. Why didn't you tell me?"

"Well, telling you that I fucked your best friend once upon a time is not the easiest thing to say,"

"I guess neither was *"I'm a hooker"*,"

"What?"

"Yeah, I know about Miami. Never pegged you as the type to sell your ass,"

"Jayson, you don't understand. I was going through some things and I needed quick money. I didn't tell you because I didn't want to relive it. I have worked too hard to leave that part of me in Miami. But when I found out you were cool with

Derek, I just knew it would come out sooner or later,"

"Naturally. So, was this just a one-time thing or…"

"Oh, Derek came back on a regular basis,"

"Bitch, if I wasn't drunk—" Derek interrupted.

"Yeah, the first time. After that, I had never seen anyone so sober. You made sure you were fresh and clean when you came looking for me, didn't you? Remember? It was almost like you thought they were real dates. There was no real problem until *someone* stiffed me one night,"

"Here we go with this again. You must not be able to count because I gave you the right amount,"

"No, nigga. Two fifties do not equal two-hundred. Go back to school," Joya countered. Before I knew it, the two of them were in a confrontation of their own, forgetting that I was standing between them. I zoned out trying to digest what was being said to me. Why did this keep happening? How was it that I was the man who always unintentionally got hooked onto all the prostitutes and strippers? I swear these women would be the death of me.

When the bickering got too much to handle, I threw my hands up and told both of them to leave. I needed time alone to think. Too much was happening all at once and I didn't have the capacity to handle it. How was I supposed to feel? I had an overwhelming sense of admiration when it came to Joya and I was completely on board with having this baby. But now I had second thoughts about everything. The Jayson I used to be would've called her out of her name and hurt her feelings something terrible. I would've made sure that she not only would stay away from me but, if she'd even see my face in her dreams she couldn't keep from crying.

I wanted to cut all ties from her. But I remembered her face. I remembered everything she had done for me in the short time that we'd been together. I remembered her showing me how much she cared on a regular basis. And I couldn't forget that. Maybe she *was* trying to leave that life behind. I could see the truth in that. But I couldn't fathom why she had to get caught.

Derek had to tell me; and he did it with such ease. He told me as if he couldn't wait to see my face when I found out he slept with my girl and soon-to-be baby's mother. He just didn't care. And that made me wonder what kind of friend he was to me.

I lied back in bed and sparked a blunt, hoping to forget. I wanted to forget about Joya, forget about Derek, forget about everything. I considered revisiting the old Jayson for a minute. Just to remember what that was like. I had a job, money, no attachments. I was a free agent. The only thing I ever had to worry about other than my mama was getting caught up with the cops. And even then nobody came knocking at my door until Nadia was killed in front of my house. *Man, this is some bullshit,* I thought.

I needed to lay low. I took a couple of weeks to reflect. I didn't associate with anyone outside of Mama and ignored Derek and Joya's relentless attempts to contact me. I really didn't have anything to say to her anyway. I still wasn't sure what I wanted to do until I thought about the baby. It had crossed my mind a time or two that it was possible for me to not even be the father. But I had become attached to that baby in such a short time, as I did with Joya, and I knew that wasn't the case. I loved my child already, and I still loved Joya. I set out to find her.

I called her on the way to her house but got no answer. When I arrived at her front door, my incessant banging and doorbell-ringing was unable to satisfy my visit. I couldn't figure out where she was. It hadn't occurred to me that her car was gone but I still didn't know why she wasn't answering the phone. I figured that she was busy and would call me back.

I sat for hours inside, outside and all around my house. I tried to occupy my time with weed, television, drinking; but nothing made a difference. Derek was still calling me several times back to back but I was in no mood to talk to him. Joya was heavy on my mind like an aneurysm on the brain. I called her again but still no answer. I threw on my Jordans and ran out the door. I went back to her house, figuring that wherever she had gone earlier that day she was sure to have returned by now. I ran past her parked car quickly and up to the porch, loudly yelling her name. After a few minutes the door finally opened.

"Dude, really!" Joya shouted. She stood in just a plain white t-shirt and tight gray sweatpants, gazing at me angrily as if I was the one to admit I was banging her best friend two years earlier. I didn't know what happened but curiosity plagued me.

"Joya! Where you been?" I began.

"Since when do you care? How many times did I call you? And how many times did you ignore me?"

"Girl," I said, inviting myself in. "Watch your tone. You know you and Derek dropped a bomb on me. I needed time, I had to think and get myself together. That's not something you want to hear about your baby's mama,"

"I know and I'm sorry. I'm really, really sorry. I didn't think you were coming back,"

"Okay, and once I calmed down I still wanted to check on you. I still love you and I wanted to make sure you and the baby were okay," I said. Joya paused and glared at the floor. Melancholy covered her when she slowly raised her head to look at me.

"Jayson, there's something I need to tell you," she said.

"What?" I wondered. I hope she didn't have any more skeletons in her closet because I couldn't take any more walks through the graveyard. I held my breath.

"I'm not pregnant anymore,"

"What happened?"

"I..." she hesitated. "I had..."

"You had a miscarriage?" I sighed. I rubbed my face with both palms before embracing Joya. She shed no tears but I could tell that losing the baby was like losing a part of her; at least that's how it felt to me. Just when I was getting used to the thought of being a father, it was taken away from me. And for the first time in a long time my heart hurt. Joya held me tightly as I kissed her forehead and the two of us fought tears.

I suddenly felt a vibration in my pocket and automatically

knew it was Derek calling me again. When I reached in my pocket for my phone the display confirmed it. I couldn't figure out what he wanted so badly that he called me non-stop for about a week and a half. Some things were just more important. I ignored the call until my phone rang again. This time it was Shawn so I answered.

"Yo, Shawn, this is not a good time. I'll call you back later," I started.

"Jay! Thank God, man. Dee's been calling you all week, bro," he replied hysterically.

"I know. And he knows why I haven't been answering the phone,"

"Well, you should've answered it anyway,"

"Why? What's going on, man?"

"It's Dee. He's over here tripping. He's got a gun and he might do something stupid. You gotta get over here quick. You're the only one that can talk to him,"

"Where?"

"His crib,"

"I'm on my way," I said and hung up the phone. I told Joya I had an emergency but I would back there to take care of her as soon as it was resolved. My headache had returned with a vengeance and I became worried all over again. Derek wasn't the type to lose his mind over nothing. Whatever it was that caused him to wield a pistol must have gotten to him on another level. And I was beginning to feel guilty for ignoring him for so long. Maybe had I answered the phone just once, this wouldn't be happening.

Ten minutes later, I whipped my truck onto Marietta St. where Derek's one-story home sat on the corner. The sky was a darkening gray and the wind was still as if it mimicked the situation. A crowd of people flooded his front lawn in fear as Derek stood in the midst of a circle waving his gun in the air. He screamed as people tried to talk to him but got nowhere. I approached the crowd and pushed my way through and peered at my best friend in the midst of a breakdown. He stood trembling and nearly crying. Every other word he pointed the gun towards us then back at himself. When I tried to get closer to him, he aimed the pistol at my head and yelled for me to back up; thunder echoing his voice.

"Derek, what are you doing?" I asked. I held my hands up although I had no real fear that he would actually shoot me. I knew him better than that.

"Back the fuck up, Jay! I'm not playing," he barked.

"Come on, Dee, stop acting crazy,"

"Don't fucking call me crazy! Nigga, I ain't crazy! Everybody else is crazy!"

"Look, man, just give me the gun and we can talk about it,"

"Now you wanna talk? Nigga, I've been calling you for over a week. You too busy with that ho to talk to me? She's more important than me?"

"I know this ain't about Joya. I *know* this. Just come in the house and talk to me," I pled. Derek stared into my eyes without blinking and motioned with the gun for me to walk inside. I lowered my hands and slowly moved as I contemplated what to say to him. Though I knew him better than anyone else, this incident was puzzling. I had never seen him fly so far off the handle. Thunder roared uninterrupted as I shut the door behind me.

The house was a mess as if the tornado brewing on the outside had already hit his living room. It smelled of a distillery that was cleaned with marijuana furniture polish. As I glanced at the dirty coffee table, I noticed a wrinkled piece of aluminum foil next to a lighter and short glass pipe with a blackened tip. It was then that I knew the cause for his mental episode. Derek paced the floor nervously, breathing heavily and rubbing the pistol with his palm.

"Dee," I called to him. He bit his nails and continued to fidget across the floor. "I thought you said you wouldn't do that shit again,"

"Hm?" he said. He glared at the table as I pointed in its direction.

51

"Dee, man, you were doing so good with that. What happened? Talk to me,"

"I'm so tired of talking. Talking never worked so now I have to do something different,"

"What are you saying? After all these years, why the heroine? I don't understand what could've been that bad,"

"Exactly, you don't understand. Little by little I'm losing everything. I already didn't have shit to begin with. They got my house, my money; my girl is gone, I ain't had family since my mama died. You were all the family I had left until you got with that ho. Man, that bitch got your nose wide open, and you forgot all about me. That's cool, I got that bitch,"

"What are you talking about? Why didn't you tell me you were having problems? You know I got your back,"

"Funny. Just when shit hit the fan that's when you stopped answering your phone. I bet you wish you didn't ignore me now," Derek formed a sinister smile.

"You're right, I do wish I answered when you needed me. And I'm sorry that I didn't, but we can work this out,"

"There's nothing to work out, Jay. It's over. I'm done. I'm sorry, man. I shouldn't have taken that from you but I didn't have a choice. Now look at me. You were all I had left, man. You were all I had left," he said. Before I could say anything further Derek turned the gun to his chest and pulled the trigger. A loud boom of thunder rang out from outside the moment the bullet left the barrel and Derek fell to the floor. My boys rushed in from outside as I was frozen. I couldn't move watching the blood slowly create a bigger puddle beneath Derek's body and his shirt turn from white to a deep red. I couldn't breathe. The moment played itself over and over again in my head while I thought to myself, what just happened?

The minute I got the feeling back in my legs I backed out of the room and ran to my car. It wasn't until I saw Joya sitting on the top step of her porch that I knew I had even started the car. As I turned off the engine, I sat in disbelief. I lowered my head and took deep breaths before tears filled my eyes. I gripped the stirring wheel when I heard the car door shut. I glanced over and saw Joya sitting next to me; I hurried to wipe my face. She placed he hand to my back.

"What happened?" she asked.

"He's dead. I tried to talk him out of it but he did it anyway," I replied.

"Who's dead?"

"Derek. He killed himself,"

"Wow. I'm sorry, baby," she said. I squeezed my eyes tightly in an attempt to stop the tears but they continued. I still couldn't get the image out of my mind. When Derek took his life he took a part of me with him. No, I hadn't been around him lately and I ignored his calls, and his messages. I felt the pain of his bullet in my chest with the guilt that took hold of my heart; and it had no intentions of letting go.

"Jayson," Joya continued. "There's something I need to tell you,"

"What?" I replied. I really didn't want to hear it, especially if it was bad. I had had enough heartache for a lifetime.

"I know it's not a good time to tell you but you need to know. I didn't exactly have a miscarriage," she confessed. I raised my head in confusion as I wanted to hear more but wasn't sure that I could take it.

"What? I'm lost. So you're still pregnant?"

"No. Something happened a couple of weeks ago,"

"Well,"

"I..." she hesitated. I wished she would spit it out already. I didn't have the patience for this confession as it was. "I had an abortion,"

"Oh, Joya. Why did you lie to me?" I whined, dropping my head onto the headrest. "You realize I wanted that baby. I would've made sure both of you were taken care of. Why didn't you talk to me about this first?"

"Well, I panicked. I thought you would leave me and I didn't know what to do. And personally, I'm not ready. We haven't been together very long and I didn't know what would happen,"

"I can't believe you," I shook my head. I didn't even want to see her face at that point. My chest tightened even more and I just wanted to be alone. I was starting to feel depressed but I wasn't sure that I wanted to be relieved of the feeling. I deserved it for how I treated Derek, but I couldn't stand mourning over the death of my unborn child either. It was bad being buried by even worse. And my mind was beginning to understand Derek's drug-induced thoughts.

6

When my phone rang I almost didn't answer. I just let the slow song play until it was about to cut itself short. I could still hear the rain hit forcefully at my window pane as it refused to cease from just three days before when Derek committed suicide. I was still coping with the thought of losing my best friend along with the thought of losing the baby that took me a minute to realize I wanted. I hadn't been this depressed since my sister went to prison. After that, I didn't have feelings for anything. But ever since Joya came into my life, everything changed. I wasn't sure that I liked that change. I loved being with her but I couldn't figure out what happened to the times when things were simple. Before I met her, I was happy. I was secure. I knew what my days were going to be like. I didn't know that the moment I stopped to talk to her would be when all Hell broke loose.

"Yeah," I answered; my voice somewhat lazy.

"Ooh, is something wrong? You sound terrible," Mama started. Seeing her name on the caller I.D. would be the only reason for me to answer my phone.

"Oh, Mama doesn't know what's up with me today? Wow, you must be slipping,"

"Get smart with me again, hear?" she threatened.

"I'm sorry, Mama. There's just a lot on my mind,"

"Like?"

"Joya, Derek,"

"What's going on with Joya and Derek?"

"Well first off, Joya had an abortion after telling me she had a miscarriage,"

"I take it that's not what *you* wanted?"

"Apparently, it didn't matter what I wanted. She didn't even talk to me about it before she up and did it,"

"Well, what's done is done. You can't continue to cry over spilled milk. She made her decision and maybe it was God's way of saying you two shouldn't have a baby right now. If you love her, you'll forgive her. Hopefully, sooner than later,"

"I guess, Mama," I said. It was hard to admit that she had a point on some level but I was still upset about the abortion. The better decision for Joya would have been to talk to me about it before she had made up her mind. I guess there was nothing I could do about it now; but I couldn't help that it angered me.

"Now what happened with Derek?" she quizzed.

"Derek's dead, Mama," I sighed. The words tasted bitter and unnatural on my tongue. It just didn't sound right. I rose from the musty sheets of my bed and walked around the stuffy bedroom.

"Oh, my God. What happened?" she gasped.

"Shot himself," I admitted. I tried to keep new tears from falling though they began to fill my eyes.

"Okay, you know what? I don't even want to know. At the end of the day, Derek chose his path and now he's in God's hands. Just pray for him, pray for Joya, and pray for yourself. You'll get through this. I know you will,"

"Thanks, Mama," I said before hanging up the phone. I took a deep breath and contemplated what I would do about my relationship with Joya. I was on the verge of washing my hands with her and the whole situation. Maybe I would take some time to be alone so I could focus on putting my life back together. A woman would only distract me. Maybe I would see if the Atlanta Falcons had any football camps or tryouts open. I hadn't seen Traycee in a while and I know I missed her terribly. Whatever I could find to take my mind off Joya, I was down for.

Even though I felt like ending it, there was no question in my mind that I felt differently about Joya than I had any of my past relationships. A part of me was holding on to her memory. Deep down, my gut was telling me that she was worth more to me than I knew and I had to get over this speed bump in order to figure that out. I had to do what I never felt like doing; work. I started to dial Joya's number nervously. I didn't really know what I wanted to say. I was about to hang up when she answered.

"Hello," she said lowly.

"What's up?" I began.

"Nothing. Just letting you calm down from the other day. I miss you, though,"

"I miss you too. You wanna come over? I need to talk to you,"

"Yeah, I'll leave right now,"

"Aight, I'll see you in a minute. Bye," I said. As I hung up the phone I tried to think about what I would say to her, how I would start. I had nothing. My mind was blank. But then again, that sounded about right. When it came to Joya I always had to speak from my heart.

I sat across from Joya on the sofa as I stared into her face. She seemed tense, though she had every reason to be. Even I didn't know what would become of this conversation. I documented her appearance into my brain while deciding how I would begin. Her head hung low with her straight hair falling over her bare face. She looked as though she had just thrown on a solid black tank top and a pair of jean shorts and flip flops. This made me feel as though she had dropped everything to be there.

"So, how you doing?" I started, watching her as she played with her fingers.

"I'm okay," she replied. "How are you doing?"

"I'll be honest with you, not so good. I've been trying to figure out whether or not to just be by myself for a while so I can get my life back on track. With everything going on, I don't think I can take much more drama,"

"So, you're saying I bring a lot of drama?"

"A little bit, yes. Before I met you I was content. I had a steady income and most importantly, I had my best friend. But I was happy to have met you because I thought you were the perfect woman. But you're not perfect. You're far from it. Instead, I find out you're this former hooker who is incapable of telling the truth but looks down on everybody else's situation," I said. My voice was calm but I meant every word I spoke.

"Is that what you think of me?" Joya asked.

"Lately, you haven't proved me any different,"

"Okay, I deserve that. But I don't look down on you. You don't seem to be like any other man I've ever met and I respect that. I just want you to get it honest because I care about you and I don't want anything to happen to you,"

"Okay, so why'd you lie?"

"I lied about the baby because I didn't know what to tell you. I didn't want you to take Derek's side just because you've known him longer or because you're mad at me,"

"What does Derek have to do with the baby?"

"You want the truth and I want to give you the truth so here it is. I didn't have an abortion. I *did* have a miscarriage because Derek raped me,"

"Don't lie," I said.

"Jayson, after everything you've found out about me the last thing I would do is lie to you. It's true. The night that he told you about Miami, he followed me back to my house where we got into an argument. I didn't care anymore that he owed me money it was just the principle of the fact. I had to tell him about himself. But he lost it, saying that he would take it whenever he wanted it and it didn't matter that I was with you. He grabbed me by the throat and punched me in the face a few times. He hit me hard enough that I almost blacked out. The next thing I remember was my clothes being ripped off and looking up at his face while he fucked me," she confessed.

"Derek wouldn't do that,"

"Maybe he *normally* wouldn't do that but he did. I swear on my life, Jayson, that's how I lost the baby. The boy was unstable," she said. It didn't sound right. Derek wasn't the type to rape anyone especially his best friend's girl. That man was my brother and it didn't make sense that he would do something so malicious. A few dollars couldn't drive him to lose it on Joya like that. My fury rose higher at an overwhelming rate. I refused to comprehend what I was being told. When I think about it, Derek had an immensely dark side to him that I wasn't fully aware of. His personal life wasn't something he discussed on a regular basis and his feelings were absent because he, himself, didn't feel he really had a heart. But when I saw him with a gun in his hand that he pointed to his own shaken self, I sensed that he'd lost control of his soul completely. He was no longer the same person I had grown up with.

I sat on the edge of the couch, lowering my head between my knees. This information was entirely too much to swallow. Now that Derek was dead I couldn't even confront him about it. However, on some level I didn't think I had to. I felt Joya's warm hands coat my five o'clock shadow as she pressed her forehead against my temple. I breathed heavily and prayed that I awake from this dream before my body exploded from the stress. Joya kissed my cheek as a tear fell from my eye. My heart was pounding out of my chest and I couldn't picture myself being away from Joya anymore. I needed to wrap her body around mine for the comfort that barely existed for me anymore.

I tried to get over the situation as much as I could in the next couple of months. Mid-September had arrived and the cool autumn weather was beginning to settle. I spent a lot of time with Joya, my mama, and the rest of my boys. While I was out searching for a new job, I went to see my sister Traycee a couple of times a week. Because the summer had passed, I'd missed out on my opportunity to join football camp for the Falcons. Instead, I signed up for the following summer and renewed my gym membership to get my body back to where it needed to be. I was always cut with defined muscles that made a shawty go crazy. But my endurance was less than desirable and my body had to get used to playing ball again. After all, I hadn't touched a football in nearly five years.

I was following a lead I had gotten for a job at a restaurant in downtown Atlanta one morning and was on my way to the gym. As I left the upscale bistro dressed to impress in a crisp white button-down shirt tucked into black slacks and black wing-tip shoes, I turned the corner to find that my truck was gone. I couldn't understand how my car had gotten stolen right out from under me. *This could not be happening*, I thought. I groaned and cursed to myself, nearly driving my fist through the concrete wall of the building I had just come from. I took a deep breath and looked up at the orange sun getting ready for the day ahead on the other side of town. I started to call Joya but remembered that she was at work and would be unreachable. I clicked the menu button on my phone to call one of my friends when the screen went blank. It was dead. *Damn!* I started off down the street to Peachtree Station and took the train until I was three blocks from home.

I literally pounded the pavement as I was mad all over again. I couldn't wait to get home and change my clothes because I would for sure be in the streets all night just hoping whoever stole my car would drive it past me. Although I had changed in a few ways, I still wasn't above taking somebody down if they stole from me. I was fired up. When my house was in view just a few yards away, I noticed a group of people coming in and out of the front door. Piles of my belongings crowded my front yard and a FOR SALE sign had been planted in the ground. My nightmarish day was turning into something even worse. I approached the stocky, young man who was standing in the back of a moving truck and demanded to know what was going on.

"I was contracted to move this stuff to a storage unit on Grayson Ave," he informed. Contracted by who? None of this really made sense.

"Look, man, this is *my* house. Who the fuck told you to move my shit anywhere? Because it sure as hell wasn't me!" I barked.

"Hey, I'm just doing my job. You should've gotten a notice in the mail about this," he said as he continued to help his colleagues pack my things in the truck. I hustled over to my mailbox and checked the day's mail as I muttered to myself, "I ain't got *shit* in the mail." I looked through the stack of envelopes and tore open one from the Atlanta Housing Authority, telling me that my house would be foreclosed since I hadn't made a payment in three months. It also told me that everything inside, including my furniture and personal items, would be taken to a storage unit; if I neglected to pay the facility all my things would be auctioned off in another three months. I threw the letter down in a rage but on some level I knew this would happen. Bills had been piling up for a while now but I thought I would've found a job by now so I just ignored them. They would get it, when I got it.

I opened up another letter I'd received that only made my blood boil even more. My car hadn't been stolen. In fact, it was repossessed. Wasn't I supposed to get more notice than this? What was I supposed to do without my car? And even worse, where was I going to live? I hated the thought of having to move back in with my mother. I was proud to be a young, black man who had his own. But now my pride had been cast down before me and there was nothing I could do about it. All the money I had stashed away had disappeared when I got arrested. It hadn't occurred to me until just then what Derek meant when he said he shouldn't have taken that from me. He must've taken my money, but for what? Why would he steal from me when he knew that I would give him the heart from my own chest if he needed it? But maybe my mind was just looking to blame anyone but myself for this mistake.

I was beginning to sweat through my shirt as both the humidity and my irritation rose. I was in a paralyzed panic because I didn't know what to do or where to go. Suddenly, my phone rang and I answered with a quickness.

"Yeah," I said. I tried to sound as together as I could but I was fighting back tears.

"So, I drove past your house earlier on my way to work. Is there something you didn't tell me?" Joya began suspiciously. What could I tell her? That my past due bills had caught up with me and that I was now homeless? I had never been so embarrassed.

"Baby, they took my house," I blurted.

"Jayson, what?"

"I ran out of cash,"

"What do you mean you ran out of cash? What happened to all that money that you were going to use for your bail?"

"I don't know. When I got out, it was gone. I have a feeling Derek might've taken it for himself but I don't know. Either way, I think I'll have to move in with my mama,"

"Jayson," Joya sighed, sucking her teeth. "You don't have to do that. I have a spare key inside the mailbox next to my front door. You can stay with me,"

"Baby, are you sure?"

"Why the hell not? Just as long as you really try to get a job so you can help me. It's hard enough trying to take care of myself,"

"Thank you so much. I owe you,"

"You can go over there now and I'll see you when I get off. My break is about over,"

"Aight, baby. I love you,"

"Love you," she said. I hung up the phone and looked up at the cotton clouds separating themselves and letting out the sunlight. I took that as God saying He was still looking out for me. While trying to gather up my clothes, shoes and other personals, I became more thankful. Being with Joya seemed so bittersweet. On one hand, my life had never been so awry. But on the other hand, Joya was always there to fix what had gone wrong. She was the disease and the cure.

Slowly but surely I seemed to be losing everything in my life but at the same time strengthening my relationship with Joya. It scared me because, based on what Derek had said before he died, my life was going in the same direction. I never had a desire to kill myself. However, neither did Derek as far as I was concerned. On the flip side I still had two women who were always in my corner with no signs of abandoning me; my mother and my girlfriend. I just had to remind them of how much I appreciated them.

I tried to make Joya forget about the fact that I was still out of work by doing little things around the house for her. When she'd come home from work, I would cook a meal to be eaten by candlelight. After rubbing her feet, I would usually have a bubble bath waiting for her and some unbelievable sex to end the night with. For a while, it kept a smile on her face. She rarely complained. But when I suddenly stopped after about a month of living together, she grew tired and suspicious.

I was sitting on the sofa lost in my thoughts when she walked in from work one evening. I heard the clicking of her stilettos on the hardwood floor as she entered the living room and stood next to the couch. I ignored her presence while my mind focused on something I felt was more important at the moment.

"Hey," she started.

"What's up?" I replied while staring at the blank television in front of me.

"Did you find a job?" she asked as she sat down next to me. I shook my head. "Hm. Well, I was wondering why you stopped doing all those romantic things for me. I thought that, maybe, you had gotten a job so you didn't have the time," she said. I didn't respond when she continued. "Did you *look*?" I snapped out of my daze and turned my head to face her.

"What are you talking about?" I quizzed.

"A job, Jayson. Did you look for a job? *Have* you looked for a job since you moved in?"

"Why would you even question that?"

"Because at first you're doing all these wonderful things for me when I come home, which I appreciate. So, I look past that one. But then it stops and I figure that you must've found one because that would be the only reason why you would suddenly stop doing those things," she said. I couldn't believe that she was angry because I didn't have dinner waiting for her. But I had other things on my mind lately.

"Don't start this shit, Joya. Please, don't start," I begged.

"Start what? All I want to know is why you haven't found a job yet. And I dare you to tell me that nobody wants to hire you because of your record,"

"Well, I'm sorry but it's true. It's a little bit harder for me. We can't all be Miss-Corporate-Job like you. And if you wanna take it there, I had a job until I gave it up for you. I was good when I was hustling,"

"Were you? Because I could've sworn you almost got locked up and if it weren't for me you'd be in prison right now,"

"Really? You're gonna throw that in my face right now?"

"Well. All I'm saying is, money is about to be even tighter around here. Because people at my job don't know how to manage their finances, I had to take a pay cut. With that being said, I'm *really* going to need your help because I cannot do it by myself,"

"Well, I'm sorry, but I'll get something when I can. End of discussion," I declared and rose from the sofa. Joya began screaming for me to stay so we could finish the conversation but I refused. She was beginning to get on my nerves and I couldn't handle any more stresses on my brain. Actually, I was so caught up in trying to dissect my issues with Derek and my missing money that finding a job had slipped my mind. It didn't matter as much. I grabbed my black sweatshirt from the other side of the sofa and left the house to clear my mind and try to put the pieces of the puzzle together. It bothered me on a whole different level that Derek was no longer able to explain himself. He was the only person who could answer the questions I had point blank. I was in search of another source.

I walked over to the spot in hopes that I would find Shawn or Jordan or even Kris so that someone might be able to tell me something about Derek. Just as my legs were growing tired I spotted Shawn's oversized black coat as his body inside leaned against the building on the corner. He was standing alone smoking a cigarette. I approached him nonchalantly.

"Hey, Shawn. What's up, man?" I said as I shook his hand.

"What's up, Jay? I feel like I haven't seen you in a while since you stopped hustling," he greeted.

"Yeah, there's a lot that's going on. It's like the shit's never-ending,"

"Right. I still can't believe what happened to Derek. I knew that fool was losing it because he was acting really strange,"

"Strange? Strange like how?" I quizzed. Shawn hesitated and looked around him.

"Aight, I wasn't gonna say anything but you can't go telling your girl,"

"Why not?"

"Because she's crazy. Look, Derek did something a while back. Nobody knows why but he was bragging about it,"

"What did he do?"

"You remember that girl that got killed by your crib?" Shawn wondered. Bubbles started to form in my stomach as I tried to figure out what Nadia had to do with Derek. And I was praying that Shawn wasn't about to tell me what I was thinking. I nodded my head in response to Shawn's question as he continued, "Well, Dee called in a few people just before she got shot. Matter-fact, the *night* before,"

"Please don't tell me Derek had something to do with that?" I pleaded.

"I wish it wasn't like that, bro. Like I said, he was bragging about getting that girl killed but he didn't say why he did it. He was cool until the niggas that did it came looking for him,"

"Why would they come looking for him?"

"See, they made a deal to kill the girl for ten grand. But at the last minute, they switched it up and asked for a hundred thousand and if he didn't pay up they would smoke him too. I already know they weren't ordinary niggas because they had Dee spooked. He was trying to get money as fast as he could and would do anything he could...*anything*,"

"Do you think he had anything to do with my money coming up missing?"

"Man, when you told him to take your shit and give it to Joya it was like you personally put that money into his hands. I just can't believe he really took it with a straight face and without hesitation. The day he went crazy and killed himself was the day they were coming for him. But he beat 'em to it,"

"That's Derek for you," I said shaking my head. I shook his hand one more time before leaving him. Shawn was only confirming what I had already suspected. The moment I gave Derek access to all the money I had to my name was the day I fueled his secrets. Finding out that he was the driving force to Nadia's death was like hitting a brick wall going a million miles per hour. I had to decide whether or not to tell Joya. She deserved to know what happened to her best friend but I still had so much annoyance swirling around in my head. I wouldn't tell her now. She would hate me for something I had nothing to do with. And we had enough problems as it was. I would tell her later when a better time presented itself.

I wasn't sure what my next move would be. I considered going back home but seriously wanted to avoid any drama awaiting my arrival. Both Joya and I needed time to blow off steam before we spoke again. As the night began to fall and I hiked amongst the bitter wind, I saw my mother's face. Without realizing it, I started to trek in the direction of my childhood home. These were the times when I needed to vent and receive some much-needed guidance. I longed to experience the moments I had as a kid with Derek and Traycee playing Tag in the front yard. Back when prison was a place I'd never heard of, strawberry Kool-Aid was considered a drug, and death was nonexistent; people just took a permanent vacation to a heavenly place. I wanted to put myself back in that state of mind before my adulthood drove me insane.

When I entered the house I immediately felt a peacefulness come over me and a subtle smile appeared on my face. The house was quiet except for the faint sound of the television in the living room. I went to join my mother but found her sound asleep on the sofa, covered in a quilted blanket. I planted a soft kiss on her cheek and headed up the stairs to my old room. It smelled just as I remembered it not even ten years earlier. My posters of LisaRaye and Tyra Banks were still in place on the wall. My football trophies were polished on the shelf around a picture of me in my uniform. I took off my Timberland boots and lay back on the jet black spread draped over my bed and closed my eyes. I entered a daydream and decided that I would feel what I felt back then even if it killed me.

I awoke to a brightened room that felt like my troubles had been lifted from my mind and heart. For a second, I thought I'd woken up in the 1990's on a Saturday morning after a big win against our rival school South Buckhead High. Well, it was Saturday and it was morning. But even being in the present I felt well-rested and ready for whatever. I wiped the crust from my eyes and went to the bathroom before going downstairs to find my mama. I walked through the living room and noticed the clock on the cable box read 11:23AM before I continued to the kitchen where my mother was standing amidst a stove-full of steaming skillets.

"Hey, Mama," I said as I kissed her. I must have startled her because she jumped back with her hand to her chest when she saw me.

"Boy, don't scare me like that. When'd you get here?" she said. I took a seat at the kitchen table as I watched her cook several things at a time. She was still in her pajamas, which consisted of a plain white t-shirt and sweatpants, and had a multi-colored satin scarf tied around her head.

"Last night," I answered.

"Last night? It must've been late if you snuck in without me knowing,"

"Not really. It was about nine o'clock. You were asleep on the couch,"

"Oh, sounds about right. What's going on, though? Why'd you sleep here?"

"I just wanted to see you,"

"That's it?" she questioned. She wore a skeptical expression as she turned off the stove and came to sit next to me. I smiled at her but said nothing. "You know I don't believe you,"

"Mama, it's nothing. Well, it's *something* but I'll figure it out," I said.

"What happened?"

"Me and Joya just got into it,"

"Got into it? How?"

"Well, she's been on my case about getting a job. But you know how hard that is when you're a nigga like me. I've been hustling all my life so I've never had a real job,"

"Honey, that just means she cares about you. She wants to see you doing well,"

"I *was* doing well before,"

"Were you? Did you forget that you're on probation and, because of her you didn't get locked up again? Lord, I prayed that I could raise the two of you better than what I have. It's bad enough having one child in jail and you're over here complaining because you have a girl who loves you enough to prevent that from happening to me again. I like Joya and I know you love her. You just need to try a little harder. Not for me or Joya, but for you," she explained. There was nothing I could say to help her understand how I felt. In my mind, Joya didn't realize the issues I still had with Derek and how important it was for me to get to the bottom of the situation. Knowing that this started with Nadia's death pulled her into it in a way that she couldn't imagine. And I didn't appreciate her talking to me as if I were a small child. However, my focus had to be on fixing things rather than letting them fester.

"Have y'all thought about living together?" Mama continued.

"We *are* living together," I answered.

"Oh wow. I swear you don't tell me anything anymore. But regardless, why don't you go home and make up with your girlfriend," she suggested. I kissed her one more time before leaving the house.

I knew being around my mother was the very thing I needed to get my mind back on track. I kept from telling her that I'd lost the house because I knew it would devastate her and the focus would be on that rather than on the issue at hand. It was clear that my mother wanted me to appreciate Joya, but I was tired of everyone implying that she was my lifeline whether it was true or not. On this day that was more fiery than the one before, I planned to reestablish my dominance with Joya. I was determined to take back control of my life and be a man about mine.

7

"We need to talk about some things," I started. I'd come back home with Joya and just got out of the shower. I was standing in front of Joya in the bedroom with only a burgundy towel around my waist; water still dripping from my hard body. Joya herself had just awakened and was wearing only a black t-shirt and nylon basketball shorts.

"Go," she said, still lying underneath the covers and clearly eyeing my glistening body.

"Are you going to talk to me or are you going to yell at me?" I asked.

"I'm sorry. I'm just irritated because I don't know how much longer I can do this by myself,"

"I understand that. But I've got you now. I'm focused. I won't let you fall. I just had to take care of some business and, after talking to my mama, my mind is restored,"

"How can I be so sure?" she said. I climbed onto the bed and crawled just inches from her face when I replied, "Trust me." I kissed her reassuringly as she pulled my face to hers. She wrapped her arms around my neck and rolled my body underneath her, mounting me like a lioness standing over her kill. I felt the bulge between my legs grow as it could no longer be hidden by the towel. Joya pressed her fingers into my chest and moved them down my stomach. As she pulled off her top, revealing her bare breasts, I caressed her hips and dampened them with my moist grip. I tugged at the waist of her shorts when she fell to her back, allowing me to pull them off.

I watched Joya as she lay back as though she hungered for it but wanted me to take control of her. I hovered over her and kissed her passionately before moving downward to gently nibble on her poised nipple. Joya breathed heavily and arched her back in ecstasy. I firmly picked her up and pulled her on top of me when she grabbed hold of my dick and placed it inside her. She rode me in soft circles until her moans got louder. Then she bounced vigorously at my waist where I felt her moisture on the inside of her thigh.

Sweat beads formed all over me as I held onto Joya's waist and pounded her body into mine. I bit my bottom lip while trying to contain myself. As I was about to let go, I stopped her and pushed her from me. I started to regain my stamina when I faced Joya to the headboard, bending her forward, and entered her from behind. I sexed her roughly when I groaned at my climax. Joya was still moaning but had yet to let out her scream of orgasmic satisfaction. I kept going until finally she came.

Joya rolled happily under the sheets before I joined her in the midst of trying to catch my breath. This was what I needed, what calmed me. It was the perfect way for the two of us to bury the hatchet and start over. What fight? What job? I knew I had silenced her; at least for now. I embraced her under my arm as she lay her head on my chest. It felt like we had gone back to when we had first started dating. Back when we were in love without knowing it. I was here for her and she knew that. And I for damn sure knew that she was here for me. We had gone back to our happy place.

I kissed Joya on the top of her head but something was still bothering me. I tried to ignore it but it picked at the inside of my brain until I couldn't stand not knowing. The last thing I wanted to do was take us out of this euphoria. But if I was going to be with Joya I had to know everything there was to know. I couldn't take any more surprises in the future so I wanted to get it all out in the open.

"Joy," I began.

"Yeah," she replied seductively.

"I need you to be honest with me,"

"I am honest with you,"

"There's something I want to talk to you about,"

"Jay," she groaned. "We just made up,"

"I know, but if we're going to be together I need to know everything. Even what you're afraid to tell me. I can't take no more surprises between you and Derek,"

"Me and Derek? Jayson, what's this about?" she wondered as she sat up. I soon did the same.

"I want you tell me about Miami,"

"Miami? Hold up, I thought Derek already told you about that. Besides, I don't want to keep bringing this up. I just want to leave it in the past,"

"Well, we have to visit the past for a minute if we're going to have a future,"

"Okay," she sighed. "What do you want to know?"

"Everything. Like, for starters, how'd you end up as a prostitute?"

"Well," she began; I braced myself. "I'm originally from Miami. I moved out of my mom's house when I was fifteen with two hundred dollars I stole from her and no place to stay. After about a week, I convinced one of my friends to let me stay with her but her parents got tired of me too and kicked me out. I started hooking to get money for food and hotels. As I got older, it got easier and I got better," she confessed.

"And how did you meet Derek?" I asked.

"About three years ago, Derek approached me one night. His car was nice so I figured he had money. When I got in, he was obviously pissy drunk but he was driving okay and I needed the cash. I asked him what he wanted and I gave it to him. I guess I made him feel like something because he came back the next night,"

"Okay, and what's all this about him owing you money?"

"Well, I saw him for like a week and a half straight. He would actually take me out to dinner and bring me flowers..."

"Derek?"

"Yes, Derek. It was like he was falling in love with me. He even bought me a diamond necklace,"

"Do you still have it?"

"I pawned it the next day," she said, shaking her head. "But anyway, the night before he left town we got into it really bad. He thought he only owed me a hundred and when I tried to tell him different he stormed out of the hotel room and I never saw him again. After that, I just couldn't deal with being there any-more so I packed up and came to Atlanta, hoping that things would be different and that I could forget about the whole thing. I wanted to reinvent myself. Then I met you and I found out that Derek was your best friend and that reinventing myself was not going to happen. And there's the full story from begin-ning to end,"

I nodded my head at her. I didn't like what I was hearing but it was what I needed to hear. It was what I asked for. In the fifteen years I'd known Derek, he had never been one to pay for a hookup. And he really never pegged me to be the type to fall in love with one. Joya had a way about her that could make any man crave her without even trying. With that being said, I could believe that he wanted her even though he hated her. But the gifts and the dinners was just unreal. I let it marinate in my head for a bit. Then I made a decision. I had to give Joya the very thing I was asking of her; honesty.

"Okay, now there's something you need to know," I continued.

"What?" she questioned.

"Don't react when I tell you this. There's nothing you can do about it anyway,"

"Jayson, just tell me,"

"Derek hired somebody to kill Nadia. Nobody knows why. The money he was supposed to give you to bail me out of jail, he stole that to pay them off. That's how I suddenly ran out of cash. The niggas that got her were about to kill him when he killed himself," I said. It came out so easily and I didn't care how upset she would get. Before we could go any further in our relation-ship, the truth had to be known on both sides.

"What?" she said. Joya's jaw dropped slowly while the rest of her body was motionless. Her eyes were paralyzed on me.

"Nobody knows who did it. But it doesn't even matter be-cause I'm sure they're long gone by now," I said.

"How long have you known this?" she asked.

"I just found out yesterday. I thought you needed to know,"

"Yeah, well, thanks. I swear, if that nigga wasn't already dead

I would kill him,"

"I believe you. Derek got lost somewhere along the lines and he made his choice. But it's over. What we need to do is focus on us. We don't need any more problems and secrets. That's why I wanted us to have this conversation," I said. Joya nodded her head as she nervously bit her thumbnail. Although I was unsure about telling her the previous night, I knew I was only making things worse by keeping it inside. She could scream, she could cry. She was open to do whatever she needed to do if it made her feel better. But at least I knew that the slate was clean for the both of us.

Fall was beginning to settle in comfortably as the wind chill dropped by the week like the leaves on the trees. I was on a hunt for a job that didn't require me to sell drugs although I was growing restless and was beginning to miss the hustle. I called in a favor with one of my high school buddies who managed Club 112 and got a job as a bartender every other night. I tried to keep my cool but I was really excited. After several months of being unemployed and feeling as though I was at Joya's mercy, I could finally do for myself again. It felt good because it meant that we could finally stop having the same argument over and over again. I felt like a grown man again.

I had borrowed Joya's car and drove straight home after receiving the news. As I entered the house, I approached Joya in the kitchen with my arms wide open. I hugged her from behind and kissed her neck as she stirred a pot of spaghetti sauce.

"You look happy," she giggled.

"Guess what?" I said.

"What?"

"I got a job,"

"Yay!" she squealed. Joya turned to face me as she kissed me repeatedly. "Tell me where!"

"I will be a bartender at Club 112,"

"Really? Can you do that?"

"What do you mean, can I do that? How hard is it to mix drinks? I drink enough to know a little something-something,"

"Oh, I am just so happy. Now you can finally help me with these bills. When do you start?"

"Tomorrow night,"

"Aw, will you be here when I get home?"

"Of course I will. But we have to make those few hours count," I smiled. I felt a huge weight lifted from my shoulders. Joya and I had made an agreement that I would use her car at night so I wouldn't have to take the train, just as long as I paid for the gas. I could do that. Knowing that I had this job gave me back a piece of my pride I'd lost when everything got taken away from me, including Derek. Though it wasn't much, it was a start at something more.

I walked the busy streets to the spot after spending my time with Joya the previous night. She had already left for work that morning and I decided I needed to spend some time with my friends since I hadn't really hung out with them in a while. The afternoon weather was cool while the sun provided a small amount of warmth so I just threw my black hooded sweatshirt over a white t-shirt and dark blue jeans. I covered my head with a black and white fitted cap until Joya could braid my hair later that night before I went to work. The moment I hit the corner I heard a female's voice call my name. I turned and saw Diamond inching towards me in a purple tracksuit and tennis shoes; the most clothes I've ever seen on her. I cursed to myself and was tempted to ignore her and keep walking. I placed my hands in the pockets of my hoodie and continued around the corner where I was headed. She called again with no signs of leaving me alone.

"What, Diamond? What?" I yelled back to her.

"Hey, boo. How you doing?" she smiled.

"Girl, I am not your boo. I do not want you,"

"Oh, Jayson," Diamond said as she rolled her eyes. "I don't want you. Let me get a blunt." She moved in closer to me but I took a step back.

"Look, I ain't got nothing,"

"Nigga, you're lying. You deal all the time, how can you not have anything?" she questioned as she popped her gum.

"First of all, I don't deal anymore. And second, if I *was* still hustling I wouldn't hook *you* up. I really can't stand you and if I never saw you again it would be too soon. Bye, girl," I said. I started to turn and walk in the other direction when Diamond stopped me again; this time blocking my path with her body.

"Hey," she continued.

"What?"

"What's up with you and that girl you're always with?"

"Are you stalking me?"

"No, I just want to know,"

"Well, that's none of your business. There's a reason why you're my *ex*-girlfriend. We shouldn't even be talking because we have nothing to say to each other,"

"Damn, you really hate me, don't you?"

"Yeah, I do,"

"And ole girl is just that much better than me?"

"You have no idea. Deuces," I said, putting up the peace sign and making my way around her. I kept straight without looking back at her. I knew I hurt her feelings on some level but that was exactly what she needed to get the hint. Diamond's very existence irked my nerves. She was like a lost puppy who thought her home was with me. It wasn't. And I didn't know what it took to make her see that.

I put my run-in with Diamond out of mind and greeted Shawn, Josh, and Jordan at the spot. I watched them support other peoples' habits while adding to wads of wrinkled cash in their pockets. The money was so fast and I missed getting it. Now I had to punch a clock and abide by somebody else's rules while Uncle Sam took a piece of my check. I was starting to wonder why I hadn't gone back to hustling. The job was dangerous but I was doing the damn thing. There was no group of dope boys like me and my crew; but now I was no longer a part of that fame. I was still seriously considering going back.

I started to catch up with my friends when the four of us fell silent. Our bodies were stiff as we watched ahead of us. Two police cars rode by slowly with every officer inside staring intensely at us. We moved our heads at the pace of the cars as I pursed my lips and gave them a head-nod. To them, we looked as though we were hiding something. But to us, they were waiting for one of us to jump so they would have a reason to beat us down before locking us up. They were always more suspect to us.

"Dick-suckers," Jordan mumbled to himself.

"Yup," I agreed. We watched them turn the corner when we continued with each other.

"That's some bullshit," Jordan said. "Them niggas are just *waiting* for something to pop off,"

"That's for sure. Hey, Jay," Josh interjected. "I see Diamond's ass is still in your face,"

"Unfortunately," I replied. "I don't know why she tries so hard. I thought if a nigga was an asshole to her she would go away, but damn. She's still coming at me,"

"Might have to get Joya on her,"

"You might be right. This shit is getting out of hand,"

"But let me ask you this," Shawn said. "You ever think about smashing that just one more time?"

"Come on, man. Would you?" I said. It may have been hard for my boys to believe but not once had sex with Diamond ever crossed my mind. Granted, she had a few tricks back in the day. But it wasn't anything special; it was nothing anyone hadn't already seen before. All Diamond had was body. And she abused it. I knew she was a stripper but my intention was to make all the brothers jealous of the fact that it was I she came home to. I'd realized that my so-called intentions blew up in my face when nobody seemed to care that she was my girl. I couldn't take niggas laughing in my face all the time. But instead of fighting with a different dude every day, I cut Diamond loose and kept it moving.

The subject of Diamond was beginning to tire me and that seemed to be all my boys wanted to joke about. The breeze was becoming continuous and making me colder than what I could bare. I said a goodbye to my friends and left in the opposite direction. Since hanging out with my friends was a bust, I headed towards my mother's house. I missed her a little, and I knew that I was comfortable enough around her to be with her all day. Even if we didn't speak to one another I could never become bored. I just didn't want to be alone.

As I sauntered up the porch steps, I was already removing my key from my pocket before shoving it in the door. I damn near slammed the door behind me while yelling for my mother. I got no answer. I moved through the house in confusion. I could hear Nancy Grace's voice echo from the living room but no one was there. The kitchen was a mess. It looked as though she had just started cooking; raw vegetables and spices surrounding a large steel pot of water on the stove. This was unlike her. Mama never left food out of the refrigerator and the television on if she was leaving the house. And her car was still parked outside. She must've run out in a hurry. But for what? And if she had to go somewhere, her care wouldn't be here. Maybe she was with someone. What the hell was I missing?

I walked out to the front porch to try and put together a logical explanation for where my mother had gone. My thoughts slowed down when I heard my name being called from my left side.

"How you doing, baby?" Ms. James said, standing at the corner of her own porch. Tammy James was my mother's best friend. They met in the second grade and grew up next door to one another. Ms. James looked after me and my sister when Mama had to work. I loved being at her house because we could do whatever we wanted as long as we were respectful to her. She stayed up with us at all hours of the night, eating junk food and watching horror movies, and made the sweetest oatmeal raisin cookies on the planet. Even as a child, I'd always thought Ms. James was a beautiful woman. She was a curvaceously thick-bodied woman with smooth brown skin, candy apple red lips, and bright eyes. Her face formed round cheeks each time she smiled. Not much has changed through the years.

"Hey, Ms. James," I replied to her, fantasizing that if I was just a few years older...

"I haven't seen you in a while," she said.

"I know right. There's been a lot going on lately. Have you seen Mama?"

"You still don't know yet? Oh, Lord, well...she's in the hospital,"

"In the hospital? For what? What happened?" I quizzed. All of a sudden I became very worried. My mother had never shown any signs of being sick.

"I was about to help her cook when she just paused and her face got tight. She started holding her chest and told me she couldn't breathe. I called an ambulance for her. I only stayed behind so I could find your number and let you know what's going on,"

"Aw, shit," I cursed to myself. I rubbed the back of my head as my heart dropped and pounded in my stomach. I didn't know what to think at this point. My mother was my everything. And if something happened to her I didn't know what I would do.

"Jayson, baby, just calm down and come with me. I'm sure everything will be fine," Ms. James said. I followed her to her midnight blue Nissan Maxima and hopped in the passenger's seat. I focused my vision through the window at the city speeding past my face. I couldn't speak. All I could do was imagine was my mother in a hospital bed, weak and vulnerable. I tried to keep my mind from believing things were much worse than what they seemed. But I didn't know much. I didn't know anything. I just knew that whatever it was, my mother may not make it.

The moment I saw the sign for Peachtree Medical Center, it all became surreal. I couldn't recall the last time I had been to the hospital for anyone. This was really happening. My mother was somewhere in this building fighting for her life. I fought back so many tears. A thousand things flooded my mind. What would I do if I lost her? I didn't even know what it was but I could already see myself at her funeral. She never pegged me as one to have any health issues. She always bragged that the only time she ever lied in a hospital bed was when she gave birth, and since she wasn't having any more kids she would never do it again. So much for optimism.

I cupped my hands and held them against my forehead as I sat in the quiet waiting room, nervously rocking back and forth. I prayed that my mother was fine. That maybe she'd just had an asthma attack or something; even though she didn't have asthma. Ms. James lightly rubbed my back while she whispered her own prayer in my ear. I checked the clock on my cell phone and I couldn't believe that only ten minutes had gone by. The shit felt more like ten hours. I was beginning to get restless when a fair-skinned older man in a white coat approached us.

"I'm Dr. Ellis, how are you?" he said, firmly shaking each one of our hands. "Who are you to the patient, Rita Adams?"

"I'm her son, Jayson, and this is--"

"Tammy James," Ms. James interrupted. "I'm Rita's sister,"

"Okay, well, I've been Ms. Adams' doctor for many years and I've never seen anything this severe,"

"Wait, what?" I said. What did he mean he's been her doctor for years? If my mother was having problems with her health she would've told me.

"Usually, she would complain about chest pain but I would always link that to her high blood pressure and prescribe something that would usually take care of that. But this call was much more serious. She has a large blood clot in her heart. It's stopping her heart from pumping normally and we have to perform emergency surgery if there's any chance of saving her life," Dr. Ellis explained.

"So what you're saying is, without this surgery, my mama's going to die?" I quizzed.

"It's likely. But I can guarantee that we have our best on the job, so we're going to do everything in our power to keep that from happening,"

"Can I see her?"

"Unfortunately, that's not possible right now. She's already in the O.R. being prepped. But once we're finished with her surgery, we'll let you know,"

"And how long will that take?"

"Maybe around eight hours. Sometimes shorter, sometimes longer. In the meantime, our receptionist Donna will give you some forms to fill out about your mother's general information and medical history. You're more than welcome to stay here in the waiting room or if you decide to go home, you can leave us a phone number and we'll give you a call as soon as she's stable," he said. I nodded my head and sat back down as he handed a clipboard to Ms. James. I covered my mouth in shock as I tried to figure out where any of this was coming from.

While I always thought she had perfect health, here this man was telling me I was completely wrong. He basically looked me in the face and told me that he knew my mother better than I did. Maybe she didn't want me to worry about her. I tried to rationalize it but there was no good enough reason for her to keep something like this from me. I remembered how she stressed to me as a child how important it was to be honest with her even if I felt I had to lie to everyone else. She repeated, "I'm your mother, and there's nothing you can say to make me not love you." It made me smile to know that she reminded her kids of how much she cared for them. But as bitter as the words tasted on my tongue, I had to admit she was being a hypocrite. It was one thing for me to keep quiet about the fact that I sold dope. Even still, I eventually told her the truth. Now the shoe was on the other foot and I didn't understand why, with something this important, she couldn't practice what she preached. I couldn't worry about that now.

I looked over at Ms. James, who had filled out majority of the paperwork when she noticed my gaze. I thought about how grateful I was to have somebody like her in my life. She was always a second mother to me and my sister.

"So, what I hear is that you have a new job and a new girlfriend," she started, trying to change the subject.

"Something like that," I said.

"Tell me about this job,"

"It's nothing major. It's just a bartender at a club,"

"Oh, okay. When do you start?"

"I'm supposed to start tonight but I don't think I'm going in. Not with Mama having surgery tonight,"

"You know what I think? I think that your mother would want you to go on with your life as if nothing is wrong,"

"Obviously. Otherwise she would've told me she had heart problems,"

"Right. She doesn't want you to worry about her because she doesn't want you to get distracted from your own life and what makes you happy. She knows you love her and she loves you more than you could imagine. And from what I hear, she really likes your girlfriend; and so do you,"

"Yeah, I guess," I thought.

"Yeah," she agreed. "I think you should go home and spend some time with your girlfriend before you go to work. You need something to take your mind off of this. Besides, I'm sure she can do something with that head of yours. If you go into work with your hair looking like that, everybody's going to know you have problems." I laughed with Ms. James and embraced her tightly. I was lucky to have all these amazing women in my life who cared so much about me. Between my mother, Ms. James, Joya, and my sister Traycee, I didn't need any more females around me. I had more than enough.

Ms. James drove me home and Joya greeted me at the door. She was still in the gray sport coat and skirt she had worn to work but her hair was pulled back in a messy ponytail. I wrapped my arms around her waist and kissed her neck.

"I saw the car pull up and I was wondering where you were. What happened?" Joya started.

"I love you," I said.

"I love you too. What's going on?"

"Mama's in the hospital,"

"What? Oh my God, why?"

"They said she has a blood clot in her heart," I said calmly. I moved past her and fell to the couch. "She has to have surgery right now and they'll call me when it's over,"

"Okay, I'm confused. If your mother's in the hospital, why are you here? We need to go be there for her,"

"It's okay. My mama's best friend is up there with her and she has my back. She'll keep me updated. Mama would want me to be with you and start my job like nothing's wrong,"

"What does that mean? Are you saying you're not even worried about her?" Joya wondered. I was surprised she would even ask.

"Of course I'm worried. I don't know what I would do if I ever lost her. I'm just saying, I need something to take my mind off this whole situation. It took me long enough to get this job and I don't want to lose it already," I said.

In reality, the last thing I wanted to do was go to work. What I really wanted was to be at the hospital in the operating room looking over the shoulder of each doctor who touched my mother. But I knew Ms. James was right. My mother was the type of person who, if she found out I'd skipped my first day of work for any reason, would put her foot so far up my ass I would be coughing shoelaces. Sometimes I couldn't understand her logic. Some things were more important than being at work. There was nothing going on in my life that was a higher priority than my mother; nothing at all. However, I could never say that she didn't sacrifice her life to make sure mine was right.

8

It was precisely eleven o'clock and a full moon illuminated the night sky. Voices filled the crowded street as people waited patiently to get inside. I pushed past the group and made my way to the bar. On the way, I took several compliments on my multi-colored Coogi outfit of the night as well as the twisted design of my hair. I began serving drink after drink while keeping a smile on my face. I spoke to some friends and other acquaintances as if there was nothing bothering me when, truthfully, I was dying inside. I thought about what Ms. James had told me about this night taking my mind off of my mother's situation. It wasn't working, though. If I would continue to feel like shit, I might as well had been at my mother's bedside. At least there I wouldn't have to fake it.

As I was shaking my mother's face from my thoughts, Joya emerged from the crowd. My body felt warm all over. She swayed towards me in a little black dress and knee-high leather boots; her cleavage slightly protruding from the V-shaped neckline. Her hair was down and a little curly, and her make-up a bit heavier than the last time I saw her. She sat on a barstool and waited for me to finish pouring a cup of Remy Red.

"There's my working man!" she smiled. "How are you feeling?"

"I'm alright," I said, shrugging my shoulders. I leaned across the bar to kiss her. "I've been trying to keep my mind off things but it's not really working,"

"She'll be alright, okay? Just try not to think about it tonight. Enjoy yourself. You won't be able to find out anything until tomorrow anyway," Joya argued. I appreciated Joya's attempt to comfort me but a part of me didn't really want to hear what she was saying. She and her mother weren't tight like me and mine, so she couldn't really understand how I felt. She had no idea how hard this was on me. I ignored the situation and rushed to the other end of the bar where I noticed a friend of mine I hadn't seen in a while. Deonte was the type of person who dropped in and out of your life on a regular basis. He had a lot of things going on in a lot of different places but you could never take it personal. I shook his hand as I was surprised to see him.

"Well, if it isn't my man Jay. What's going on, boy?" Deonte started.

"Not a damn thing. It's been a minute," I replied.

"Yeah, it has. I heard you got a baby on the way. Congratulations,"

"Nah, it ain't true. What you been up to, though?"

"Same shit. Just came down to see my kids. You still play football?"

"Nope," I shook my head. "I haven't been in the game for a while. I'm thinking about starting again, though,"

"Yeah, you should. You were mean on the field, boy,"

"I guess, man. Aye, let me introduce you to my girl," I said. I motioned for Deonte to follow me back down to the other end of the bar where Joya was still sitting; now sipping on a Pineapple Malibu. As I begin to introduce the two, I spotted Diamond on her way towards the bar. I cursed to myself.

"Damn, here comes Diamond," I said. Joya and Deonte turned their heads quickly and watched her as she watched me. She wore a very short, snow white strapless dress, leaving little to the imagination. If I hadn't known any better, I'd say that she wanted to get--and keep--my attention. For the first time I didn't care that her ass was hanging out or that her chest was up high enough to put her own eye out. I just closed my eyes and wished she would change her mind and walk the other way; or at least fall down where she stood. Diamond leaned over the bar in between Joya and Deonte as if to metaphorically give them the finger.

"Hey," Diamond said. I didn't respond. I looked at Joya, whose face was twisted in disgust. "I didn't know you worked here,"

"Excuse me?" Joya interrupted, "But the three of us are in the middle of a conversation,"

"Well, he's the bartender and I'm thirsty so you figure it out,"

"Yeah, you're thirsty alright. Keep talking that trash, Mama..."

"Whatever. Anyway, Jayson, you need to stop playing these games with me. You know you miss me and the ways I used to put it down on you," Diamond said. Joya's eyes got wide when she stood to face Diamond.

"Alright, now, you're doing a little too much. You need to back up," Joya barked.

"And who the fuck are you?"

"Don't play dumb, bitch, you know exactly who I am. And if you keep testing me I will make sure you never forget,"

"Fuck you, bitch. Who are you? Clearly, you don't know who you're talking to,"

"Bitch, you ain't nobody,"

"Do something then, trick!" Diamond provoked. Without hesitation, Joya bashed her palm in the center of Diamond's face. She grabbed a fistful of Diamond's hair with one hand and smacked Diamond in the face with the other. Diamond waved her arms as she tried to control Joya's hands. It seemed as though the Devil was unleashed from Joya's body. It looked as though each time Diamond gripped a piece of hair, Joya got even angrier, which only meant she would fire back even more forcefully than the last time. A crowd had formed so happily entertained and I continued with my stance behind the bar with full view of the chaos taking place in front of me.

The moment that I was beginning to feel shame for the situation, two large security guards pulled the women apart. Diamond had a bloody lip and Joya's makeup was smeared, but both had unkempt hair and were out of breath. They cursed each other out as the guards led them through the crowd, disappearing outside of the building. I shook my head in awe. I truly never thought it would go that far. I also thought about how different I felt. I was embarrassed. Most men would be excited to have two beautiful women fighting over him. But for me, I knew Joya could've handled it better. Diamond was drunk and, as usual, talking out of her ass. I expected her to taunt Joya. But Joya was much more mature than that. I guess you can take the girl out of the street...

By 3am, I was hot and exhausted, sweating from every crevice of my body. I wiped down the bar before leaving the trashed room and started off down the street towards the train station. I relaxed in the backseat of the nearly empty train car, struggling to stay awake. The only thing keeping me awake was the violent vibration of the locomotive. A chill ran down my spine when I suddenly started thinking about my mother again. I hadn't thought about her for majority of the night after Joya's brawl with Diamond. My stomach tightened. I tried not to think of how bad it could really be. I couldn't help but to remind myself of when the doctor told me how this wasn't the first time she's had chest pains. Had this never happened, my mama could've died one day and I would've never known why. The thought made my head hurt. I wiped my eyes and hoped that I could keep my composure until I found out what the surgery had actually done for her.

Shortly after getting off the train, I stopped by the liquor store and picked up a pack of Newport cigarettes. I didn't usually smoke cigarettes but since I was no longer getting high I needed to find an alternative. As I walked nonchalantly down the quiet street, I lit the white stick and sucked anxiously on the filter. I let the cool breeze dry my slow-forming tears and inhaled the nicotine deeply. I didn't know what else I could take. New stress was building on top of the old stress I had a terrible time letting go of. I couldn't lose someone else close to me. First my sister, then my child. And to lose Derek, only to find out that he had changed into someone whose life I didn't want to be a part of, it made me sick to my stomach. And no matter how much I tried, I couldn't help but to dwell of the negativity that haunted me. All I heard inside my head was, *My mama might not make it.*

By the time I had arrived home, it was sometime after four

o'clock and I was down two more cigarettes. Joya was sound asleep in bed so I quietly took a shower before changing into only a pair of black sweatpants and slipping into the bed beside her. However, now I was unable to fall asleep. My eyes burned from exhaustion but I was wide awake with my mind racing. I lied on my back and stared at the ceiling, trying to convince myself that God wouldn't allow my heartache to continue. It would get better. It *had* to get better.

I awoke to a brightened room and realized that at some point I'd actually gotten to sleep that morning. I wiped my tired eyes and managed to get to the bathroom. Still half asleep, I used the toilet and immediately turned on the faucet. I splashed the arctic water over my face to wake me up and stared at myself in the mirror. I looked stressed and aged. I shouldn't have felt this old. I shouldn't have felt like my adulthood was taking complete control and keeping me from enjoying life. Something had to give.

I wiped my face with a bath towel and slowly made my way downstairs. Joya seemed to be M-I-A but left a note in the kitchen that she was going to the grocery store and would be back soon. I noticed that the time on the microwave was 2:15 PM and I was quick to wonder if my mother had made it out of surgery yet. A part of me just wanted to wait for the call but I didn't think I had the patience. I wanted to make sure that I was the first person to know what happened the very moment it happened. I rushed up the steps and headed straight for the shower. I dressed in bright yellow and money-green hoping to be optimistic; thinking that if I didn't wear black I wouldn't give myself the chance to be in mourning. I called Joya before walking out the door to let her know where I was going since I knew I'd be gone for a while.

"Hey, babe," Joya answered.

"Hey, I'm just letting you know that I'm about to be gone for a while," I said.

"Where are you going?"

"To the hospital,"

"Oh, have you heard something?"

"No, but I can't wait here anymore,"

"Well, I'm on my way home so wait for me so I can go with you,"

"Okay, I'll be here," I agreed before hanging up. I took a deep breath. I realized that I hadn't eaten but knew that I wasn't hungry. I didn't feel like forcing myself to eat because I knew it would be a waste of time. I just wanted to go. Joya could've showed up in two seconds and she still would've taken too long. If I didn't know something soon I was going to explode. After about fifteen minutes I was getting restless and couldn't take it anymore. I shot up from the couch and was heading out the door when Joya pulled up. It was a good thing she showed up when she did because as much as I would've loved her to be there with me, I was about to leave her ass. I helped her carry the trunk-full of grocery bags into the house and rushed her to go right back out. She could only be understanding of my anxiousness but I could tell she was annoyed by the way she scoffed as I took her car keys from her and jumped in the driver's seat.

My foot fell heavy on the gas but I was trying not to speed. The last thing I needed was to get pulled over. I didn't speak. I watched Joya out of the corner of my eye, nervously staring at me as if she was afraid I was losing my mind. I just might have been. I was weaving in and out of traffic and taking back roads, trying to get to the hospital the quickest way I knew how. I cursed to myself when Joya spoke up.

"I wonder how much this whole thing is going to cost," she said. I guess she called herself breaking the ice but, to be honest, I wanted to choke her out just knowing that was the first thing to come to her mind.

"Excuse me?" I started. "Is that really where your head is?"

"What? I can't wonder? Look, I care about your mother too but when it comes down to it, the bill will be all they think about. Let's be realistic. How *are* you going to pay for this?"

"Insurance! Shit, I don't fucking know! I don't care right now," I argued.

"I understand that but do not yell at me! I know you're scared, but damn, I didn't make this happen. I just want you to be mentally prepared for everything this comes with,"

"I hate it when you do that,"

"When I do what? What are you talking about?"

"When you talk to me like I'm a fucking kid. Who made you queen of the world? You don't know every fucking thing and I'm not that stupid that you have to hold my hand all the damn time,"

"For real, Jayson? The last thing I *want* to do is hold your hand. The problem is, you do certain things when you know better. If I talk to you like you're a child it's because you're acting like one. Think like an adult and act like one,"

"Just stop fucking talking to me right now, Joya," I said. Her voice was beginning to get on my nerves. I tried to ignore her for the rest of the drive but each time I realized that she was still in the car, it made me more upset. I really thought she had more class than that. She knew that I was dealing with a lot and for her to start this shit was not helping. The least she could've done was wait until the bill came, not before we knew whether or not my mother was still alive. That was a low blow. And I really had to keep myself from hemming her up before the ride was even over.

It was about time when I finally pulled up to the hospital and drove recklessly to find a parking spot. I barely waited for Joya as I jumped out the car and headed for the double doors. I nearly ran to the front desk and asked the receptionist where my mother was. The woman informed me that she was still in surgery on the fifteenth floor but would call the receptionist desk to let them know that I was there waiting for an update. In the meantime, I would ride the elevator to the fifteenth floor waiting room and hope that somebody could tell me something soon.

Joya followed closely behind but still I refused to speak to her. I sat in the far corner and cupped my hands to my chin where I waited. Joya took the seat next to me when she rested

90

her head on my shoulder; I still faced forward.

"Jayson, I'm sorry," she began. "I had no business bringing that up. I didn't mean for that to happen. I'm really sorry." I heard her plea for forgiveness and accepted it with a kiss to the top of her head. But I was still angry. Emotions flooded my thoughts and rational thinking was too far away for me to recognize. I needed someone in my corner and, at the moment, had no one else. The waiting seemed as if it would never cease while the current hour faded. I rubbed my head and drug my nails across my braids as a clear sign that I was going crazy. I just couldn't lose my mama. Not now. I was losing too many important people in my life. And it wasn't until then that I thought about Traycee. As strong as she was, I wasn't sure that she could handle losing our mother either. It was clear that Mama was disappointed in Traycee for putting herself in her situation. But she still had Traycee's back just as much--if not more--than I did. But when we thought about it, who else would? I didn't think I had the heart to tell her that our mother was dead; only because I felt like I wouldn't be able to keep my composure. I prayed that I wouldn't have to find the words.

After an hour and a half, Dr. Ellis appeared from the long hallway. My head was focused on the ground so I didn't notice him until I felt Joya lightly pat me on the arm. I rose quickly to meet him halfway and hoped that he gave me some good news.

"Dr. Ellis, remember me? Jayson Adams, my mother is Rita James?" I started worriedly.

"Of course, Jayson. Good news. We've just finished with her surgery and it went extremely well. We're moving her to a private room now to stabilize and you can see her in just a few minutes. Just so you know, she may need someone to look after her at first because she will be short of breath quite often, she'll have several doses of medication to take daily; about half will help her to recover and the other half will be to maintain the performance of her heart," he informed. I nodded as he continued. "It should only take her a few weeks to get back to her normal self, but the more she takes it easy, the better. Do you have any questions for me?"

"No, not at all. Thank you so much," I said gratefully.

"As a matter of fact," Dr. Ellis continued, looking at his watch. "They should be finished moving her by now so if you like, you can follow me to her room,"

"Oh yes, that would be great. Thank you,"

"No problem. Follow me," he said. I let out a sigh of relief as Dr. Ellis led Joya and I to an elevator around the corner from the waiting area. I couldn't help but to get on my knees in my mind and thank God for keeping my mother with me. I couldn't express how grateful I was to hear that she was okay. Finally, something tremendous had occurred lately. I held Joya's hand tightly. Even though I was still a little upset, it seemed as though majority of my anger had gone away. It was obvious that I was ridiculously stressed out and I couldn't control myself. But all I cared about was now two doors down and just the thought of seeing her made my stomach turn. I was afraid that she would look frail and lifeless, like she would die at any moment. I wasn't used to that. My mother had always been vibrant and alive. Forcing her to settle into a quiet life would alone kill her.

We entered the calm room where the only sound filling the air was the beeping of the heart monitor attached to my mother's body. She lay back in the bed, propped up at a 45-degree angle, as she was engulfed in a Sudoku puzzle book. She greeted us with a wide smile and, to be honest, I wanted to start crying. I had never been so happy to see her in all my life. She wasn't lifeless at all. She looked as though she was bored and ready to leave as soon as they gave the okay to do so. I don't blame her. I couldn't wait to hug her and take her home. Without realizing it, I dropped Joya's hand and rushed to my mother's bedside. I wrapped my arms around her and kissed her forehead when she spoke.

"Hi babies," she greeted. Her voice was clear and filled with happiness. "I'm so glad to see you,"

"I'm just happy you're okay," I told her. Dr. Ellis proceeded to check her vitals.

"Of course I'm okay, why wouldn't I be?"

"Mama, why didn't you tell me you had heart problems?"

"Because I knew you would worry about me and I'm fine,"

"You're in the hospital, Mama,"

"It was just a little surgery. I'm okay now. If you and Traycee and y'all's father couldn't kill me, honey..." she joked.

"So, it's clear you're feeling alright then?" Dr. Ellis interjected.

"Don't I look like it? When can I go home?" she asked.

"Probably in a couple of days. We need to keep you to be sure that everything is okay,"

"Mm hm, you just want my money," she teased. "Joya, how are you? Nice to see you again,"

"I'm good, Ms. Rita," Joya answered.

"I hope so. Come hug your mother-in-law. Don't be afraid, I don't bite," she laughed. I'd never heard her call herself Joya's mother-in-law and I found it somewhat amusing. Did she know something I didn't know? I hadn't really thought about marrying Joya any time soon and if she knew what we were really going through she would understand why. Not to say that Mama would completely disown Joya; she's always been understanding. However, she would understand my hesitation. But this was a conversation for a different time. I was focused on only my mother. Dr. Ellis left the room and I tried to let it go and change the subject. I told Mama about my first night at the club and how relieved I was to finally have a job of some kind. I would try to find one that paid more when I got the chance but I wanted to be thankful and take advantage of this opportunity. Before I could find something else to talk about, Mama brought up the subject of marriage again.

"Mama, I don't want to talk about this," I pleaded.

"I know, but I just want the two of you to get married and have some pretty little babies. Ooh, your babies will be so gorgeous. I want to have some grandbabies to spoil," she said.

"That's fine, Mama, but me and Joya will do that when we're

ready,"

"Joya, do you want to get married?"

"It would be nice," Joya replied.

"And do you want kids?"

"Yeah, one day,"

"Well, there you go, son,"

"Mama," I begged. I wished she wouldn't push so hard.

"You know what I think? I think you want to get married but you're afraid to. But that's okay, you'll do it on your own time," she said. I shook my head. As if I didn't feel enough pressure. It's not that I was afraid. I wasn't afraid of anything. Joya and I had been together for only four months and had more than enough to learn about one another. It didn't matter that I loved her. It didn't matter that she loved me. All that mattered was the fact that every time I turned around I was finding out something new about everyone I loved. I wasn't sure I really knew anyone anymore, so I was determined to take my time and figure it out. Yes, I wanted to be with Joya at that moment but who was to say that I wouldn't find out something else about her that I wouldn't be able to forgive so easily? At this point in our relationship I was an open book. There was nothing about me that Joya didn't already know. It irked my nerves to think about it. I felt like an addict as I kept telling myself, just one day at a time.

9

It was the second week of January and I was completely caught up in taking care of my mother. Joya and I had spent the holidays with her; which she didn't seem totally happy about seeing as how I refused to let her drink alcohol. "Who gave birth to who here?" she complained. The snow was settled in a comfortable and a cold front hit the city hard every morning and night. A dry breeze filled the air as snow flurries fell softly on my face. I was sitting on the top step of my mother's porch as I smoked a cigarette and thought about my visit with Traycee earlier that afternoon. My sister looked like she kept herself together but jail had still taken a toll on her. She was happy to see me but wasn't surprised that Mama refused to go. She knew our mother loved her but couldn't take seeing her in prison. The thought made Traycee emotional. She fought back tears because she took it that Mama didn't want to see her. That was far from true. My mother missed her terribly. She talked about how much she wanted to hold her daughter again but at the same time she repeated how that would never happen. It broke my heart and I promised her I would make sure they were together again.

The moment I put my cigarette out, Joya approached me. She was bundled up as if trying to hike through the middle of a blizzard. Her gold and black winter coat was buttoned to her neck as she wore a black toboggan, gloves, and black snow boots over faded gray jeans. She'd wrapped a tan scarf around her neck to top off her winterish look. I immediately rose to greet her with a kiss.

"Damn, are you cold?" I said sarcastically; a cloud of fog forming in front of my face.

"Oh, shut up. Mama inside?" she asked.

"Yeah, she's in there,"

"Did you go see your sister?"

"Yeah. She's doing really good. I just wish Mama would've

gone. And I wish you would've gone,"

"Well, I'm sorry. You know I had to work. I'll go with you next time. I do really want to meet her,"

"I know," I said. Just then, my phone began vibrating from inside my pocket. I answered it. "What's up?"

"Yo, man, I've been trying to get ahold of you. Where you been?" Jordan started desperately.

"I was visiting my—"

"Look," he interrupted. "It doesn't even matter. I need you to help me with something,"

"I already know what you want and I'm done with that,"

"It's not like that. Just get to the spot, homeboy," he demanded and hung up. I took a deep breath and looked at Joya.

"Let me use your car?" I asked.

"No, Jay. I need my car," she said.

"I'm just going up the street,"

"Then you can walk. I really didn't plan on staying long enough for you to take my car to God knows where for God only knows how long,"

"Damn, I miss my car,"

"You and me both," Joya smiled and kissed me on the lips before walking inside the house. I started off down the street and wondered what Jordan could possibly need me for that badly. I was hoping that he hadn't planned on trying to convince me to get back into the drug game. I was firm on leaving that life behind me. Jordan knew that. However, he was one of those friends who was relentless when it came to trying to get me to do things I was dead-set on not doing. I know he didn't want me to make a run for some work. And I know he didn't need me to help him make a trade. Unless it was a large trade for enough drugs that he couldn't handle it on his own. Either way, the eagerness in his voice was never a good sign.

I saw Jordan just a few yards in front of me at the spot when he turned anxiously like he had been awaiting my arrival for several hours rather than twenty minutes.

"Dude, what took you so long?" he began, slowly jogging towards me.

"Nigga, please. It ain't been that long," I argued. "What is so important?"

"Look, I need you have my back on something. This kid that took over the corner for me—"

"Woah, you're recruiting kids now?" I joked at his desperation. Jordan never broke from his original crew to bring in new muscle.

"Well, I needed somebody to take your spot. Anyway, I go to count the money from him and come to find out, he smoked up everything. See, something told me not to give him nothing more than weed," he complained.

"So, what's that got to do with me?" I wondered.

"I need to teach him a lesson. So, I need you to help me and the fellas jump that little nigga,"

"Nah, man, you don't need me to get involved with that,"

"Yes, I do. I gotta roll up on him deep and scare him shitless. And to be honest, he's a kid but he's got some muscle on me. Now, you're the sexy, flexi-ass nigga in the gym all day so I know you can do some real damage. These other niggas are just here for intimidation," he said. I looked around at the group of familiar faces who had no idea that their strength was being downplayed right in front of them. The sun was beginning to set and I wasn't certain that I felt like getting mixed up in something like this. But Jordan practically begged me and I could remember the times when I needed him to help me out in a ghetto bind. Because of this factor, I agreed to help him out. But I still was afraid this may have been a bad idea. I thought about how Joya would react if she'd found out. I knew that she would give me an earful and I would never hear the end of it. I had to be discreet and make sure that this incident stayed to myself.

I stood outside with Jordan for two hours cold, agitated, and ready to leave him where he stood. The wind had picked up nearly an hour before and I was beginning to become numb to the cold. I was about to walk away when Jordan patted my arm and pointed out that the bulky teenager walking across the street was the kid we had all been waiting for. It was about time. I was ready to get this thing over with. The five of us glanced around for police before rushing him. He started to run away but we caught him and pounded his body to the ground. The boy cried in pain as I knelt down and repeatedly punched him the face. I rose and backed away from the crowd as he held his stomach and the rest of the boys continued to batter him. My conscience was starting to take over. It was clear that they enjoyed what they were doing. Me, on the other hand, wasn't exactly satisfied with causing physical harm to some young kid I didn't even know. I was beginning to regret what I'd done. But I couldn't take it back now, I could only walk away.

I took Joya's car to work that night and it was definitely a nice break from walking and taking the train. It was a slow Tuesday night so that meant not much business. I was happy that I hadn't run into Diamond but I did allow a few ladies to buy me a couple of drinks. I didn't mind a little harmless flirting considering the fact that I had no plans to sleep with any of them. A free drink is a free drink. And after the night I'd had I needed one.

I left the club a little tipsy and went straight home. Joya was sound asleep in bed and after taking a hot shower, I was too. I started to ask God to forgive me for helping Jordan jump that young kid earlier when I fell asleep into a disturbing dream. I pictured a pregnant Joya surrounded by a sea of young children with no faces happily playing with one another in a field of violets. It was a beautiful day as I approached the group with a wide smile on my face. Suddenly, Diamond appeared from a distance. She blocked the bright sun as she approached us. She was naked. Her hands were behind her back and she showed no emotion on her face. As her eyes squinted, she pulled her hands from behind her back, wielding a twenty-two millimeter handgun. Diamond pursed her lips as I stared at her in wonderment. Joya and the group of children couldn't see her. I screamed at Diamond but no sound came out. Before I could reach her, she shot one round into my chest. As I fell to the ground, she shot a bullet into Joya's head then the head of every child around her. Once Diamond had completed her kill, she broke into guilty tears.

I woke up in a cold sweat. I wiped the sweatbeads from the back of my neck and struggled to catch my breath. I didn't know what to make of this nightmare. What did it mean? Were the kids in the dream mine? If so, why had Diamond murdered my entire family? And why was she naked? I shook my head. Maybe it didn't mean anything. Maybe this was just a figure of my imagination. Maybe it was just a stupid dream. Whatever it was, it kept me up the rest of the night. After so much tossing and turning I gave up and lied on my back and waited for the sun to finish rising. Before I knew it, I was awakened by my cell phone ringing on the nightstand. I checked the time to show a little after eleven and looked to my side to notice that Joya wasn't there. I guess I had drifted off at some point.

"Hello," I answered in a groggy voice.

"Hey, Big Head. Why didn't you tell me Mama was sick?" a familiar female voice said. *Mama?*, I thought. I know this is not my sister on the other end of the phone. There was no way.

"Whoa, who is this?" I questioned.

"Who *is* this? You don't recognize your baby sister's voice?"

"Traycee?"

"The one and only. Now, wake your ass up!"

"Yo, where are you calling from? I know you can't call cell phones from jail," I asked.

"I'm at Mama's. And you never answered my question. She just told me she was in the hospital a while ago. You could've told me when you came to see me yesterday," she barked. This could not have been happening. Was my sister really out of jail? It wasn't normal practice to let someone out after four years when their sentence was well over twenty. I was confused. Had she broken out? There was a warm feeling that covered me but I was still a bit concerned.

"Tray, I didn't tell you because I didn't want you to be worried about it. Listen to me, I sound like Mama. Look, I'm sorry, sis. When'd you get out? How'd you get out?" I wondered.

"We'll talk about that later. I wanna see you, bro,"

"Of course. Let me take a shower and I'll be there in a little bit,"

"Okay, love you,"

"Love you too, sis," I said, hanging up. I jumped from the bed and swiftly ran to take a shower and get myself together. I was shaking with nervous excitement and wanted to scream at the top of my lungs. It was like my best friend reappearing from the dark after so long. I ran out the door and headed to my mother's house as quick as a cheetah runs after its prey. The second I'd arrived, I pushed through the front door of my mother's home and entered the living room where I laid eyes on my sister. She was cleaned up, looking absolutely beautiful in a skin-tight peach-hued t-shirt, a pair of dark designer jeans, and some white Air Jordan sneakers. Her hair was pulled back in a low ponytail and her face was without make-up. My baby sister was now a full grown woman who no one could tell had just been released from prison.

The moment our eyes met a wide grin grew on our faces as Traycee ran and jumped into my arms. I picked her up off the ground and held her tightly as I took in her scent. She squealed my name in my ear while her thin arms gripped my neck. I tried to blink back the tears forming in my eyes but the moment Traycee began to sniff I couldn't contain myself. There was no way to really explain my joy. I hadn't felt this kind of happiness in a long time. Even after meeting Joya, there was still a hole in my heart that formed the moment I found out Traycee was on her way to prison. But now I could say that the hole had been filled and my heart was complete again.

I kissed my sister on the forehead when she playfully pushed me away.

"Don't think I'm not still mad at you," she said.

"About what? What did I do?" I questioned.

"You didn't tell me about Mama,"

"I said I'm sorry. When did you get out?"

"Last night. I was going to show up at your house until I saw that wasn't your house anymore. Seems like you're keeping a whole lot of secrets from me lately, huh?"

"No, that's not what I was trying to do. I'm fine so there was really nothing to worry about. It wasn't worth discussing anymore. Listen, did they let you out?

"You could say that?"

"Seriously, I know you weren't stupid enough to break out?"

"So, who's this new girlfriend and when do I get to meet her?" she changed the subject.

"Her name is Joya. She's at work right now but I'll bring you by the house or bring her by when I can," I answered, even though I knew she was trying to avoid the question. I would for sure bring the subject back up at a later time.

"So, is that where you're staying? Huh, huh, huh?" she asked while playfully punching me in the arm.

"Yes, Traycee,"

"Aww, my brother is in love. That's so cute," she said in her best baby voice while rubbing my cheeks.

"Shut up," I said with embarrassment.

"Well, come tell me what's been going on. I'm surprised I haven't seen Derek around here. Has he finally come to his senses and stopped acting like he's the American gangster?" she joked. I didn't expect Traycee to ask about Derek so quickly even though she was just as used to seeing him as I was. The two of them had an odd relationship. It was as though they were big brother and little sister but at the same time were flirtatious with each other. I'm sure Traycee knew that I wouldn't exactly condone a relationship between her and my best friend so she never took it any further. However, I would've preferred that union over the one that got her locked up in the first place. Either way, I didn't want to be the one to tell her that Derek was gone.

"Tray, Derek passed away," I said. The words were still painful for even my own ears to hear out loud.

"Damn, what happened?" Traycee wondered sorrowfully.

"He killed himself,"

"Oh, my God. But why?"

"It's a long story. I don't even wanna get into it,"

"Were you there?"

"Right in front of him. I couldn't stop him,"

"I'm sure you tried, though,"

"Yeah, I really did," I said. I held Traycee close as a single tear fell from her eye and she quickly wiped it away. I led her into the living room and sat beside her on the sofa to continue our conversation, hopefully outside the subject of Derek.

"Are you okay?" I asked her.

"Yeah, I'm fine. So...you said her name is Joya?" she changed the subject again.

"Yeah...Joya,"

"That's pretty. How long have y'all been together?"

"A little over six months now," I thought.

"Do you love her?"

"Yeah, I do,"

"She's not a stripper or a hoodrat is she?"

"No, Traycee, she's not,"

"And she loves you?"

"Yeah, she does. And get this, she sort of talked me into trying out for the Falcons,"

"Oh, you're gonna play football again? That's good," Traycee screamed. Her eyes lit up and she looked at me like a little girl gazing at her father in admiration. I smiled back at her, taking in just how surreal the moment was for me. As much as I was enjoying it, I had to let the cat out of the bag.

"Traycee, tell me the truth," I started.

"The truth about what?" she wondered.

"Tell me how you got out. And don't lie to me and say they let you out because if they did you would've told me when I asked you before,"

"I didn't hear you before,"

"Keep lying to me..." I threatened.

"I got released, okay. I'm not lying,"

102

"How?"

"I don't know. All they told me was that my conviction got overturned and let me go. I don't know anything else. Really, I don't even care," she told me. I stared at her in suspicion because I wasn't sure that I could believe her. Something didn't add up. My sister had never really been one to lie to me about anything but one thing I knew well was the legal system. There was much more to this than I knew. It was apparent that I was ecstatic knowing that I'd gotten my little sister back. But I still had to find out how this happened. I stared at Traycee in suspicion. She stared back as if to say, "What? I don't know what you want from me." I didn't know who could tell me the real story-- if she was in fact lying--so I decided to let it go and enjoy the fact that my sister was finally home.

The lights were dimmed as Traycee and I reentered our mother's home. I drowned out police sirens passing by while trying to focus on the task at hand. The house was quiet. As I turned up the lights in the living room, a crowd of family members and my sister's close friends sprung from behind the furniture to scream a "Welcome home" message to Traycee. I hugged my sister and kissed her cheek as she grinned from ear to ear. She looked around as the house had been decorated with different colored balloons, streamers, and a personalized banner. A double chocolate cake had been set in the center of the coffee table. Tears forced themselves from Traycee's eyes while she buried her head into my chest and sniffed heavily. She suddenly broke from our embrace and began to greet the barrage of guests who had clearly missed her.

I kissed my mother before moving towards Joya and pulling her in Traycee's direction. Joya was stunningly dressed in a white and violet pencil skirt dress and black stilettos that she'd worn to work earlier that day. I placed my hand on the small of her back as I started to introduce them.

"Tray, this Joya. Joya, this is my sister Traycee," I smiled.

Traycee quickly wrapped her arms around Joya and hugged her tightly.

"Hi! It's so good to finally meet you," Traycee squealed.

"It's good to meet you too," Joya said. "Welcome home,"

"Thank you. Oh my gosh, I can't believe how pretty you are,"

"Well, thank you,"

"You're welcome. I'm so glad you came. I know I don't know you but it really means a lot to me,"

"Oh, it's no problem. I know how much you mean to Jayson so it's my pleasure to come and be a part of this,"

"Oh, I like you already," Traycee said. Suddenly, Shawn approached her from behind and gently nudged her shoulder. She excitedly jumped into his arms while I smiled at the two of them interacting. It seemed that Traycee was just as cool with my friends as I was. They all adopted her as their little sister in a way that made me feel like she always had someone to protect her even when I wasn't around. However, my baby sister also had a reputation as a big flirt. She drew the attention of many men--including my boys--with her beauty and down-for-whatever personality. Every man wanted a woman who could party like a man and love like a woman; and I hated to admit that Traycee was such a woman. I worked overtime to keep the dogs away from her kitty cat.

I was noticing the way that Shawn smiled at Traycee. He lightly touched her elbow and played with her hair. Traycee reacted in a way no different than she did towards me. I thought that even if he had a secret crush, I could tell she didn't really feel the same way and swept the issue under the rug. At times, I had to let Traycee take care of herself but was always a shadow behind to ensure her safety. But Shawn wasn't that type of man. I sipped straight vodka as I ignored the situation and mingled with other guests. I'd introduced Joya to a group of cousins I hadn't seen in a few years and, before long, was boasting about how much I loved her and wanted to marry her. It was clear to everyone that these were tipsy words, though Joya watched me with surprised eyes. Her expressions ranged from confusion to happiness to embarrassment, and at times it looked as though she didn't believe a word I was saying. And on some level neither did I.

10

A pounding beat through my head like a determined hammer on a nail. My eyes closed even tighter as I attempted to ignore the noise, which seemed as though it was the bass line from a song. I tossed and I turned through the bed sheets until it finally stopped. I could feel the contents of my stomach sit nearly at my throat. The previous night was epic for my family but chemically nightmarish for myself. One glass of New Amsterdam vodka turned into two bottles and six shots of brandy. I had never gotten that drunk...at least not in front of my mother, and I was surely feeling the after-effects hardcore. As I was in the middle of promising God that I would never drink again if he took the pain away, I started to hear a male voice coming from downstairs. I slowly stepped out of bed holding my head and suddenly wondered how I'd changed into a pair of black silk pajama pants on my own last night. I hesitated going down the steps while I heard Joya's voice joined with the unfamiliar man. The conversation was heated. I approached the bottom of the stairs to find a tall, lanky man taunting Joya. He was refusing to leave as she cursed him out. I quickly intervened.

"Yo, what the fuck, man?! You gotta get up out of here!" I demanded. I didn't have a clue who he was but he was clearly disturbing the peace in my house.

"Man, fuck you!" the man said.

"Hey!" Joya interrupted. I laughed as I said, "Joy, you better get him. That nigga don't know me,"

"Babe, go back upstairs. I got this," she continued. She placed both hands on my bare chest, trying to nudge me in the direction of the stairs.

"I don't know who the hell you are but you need to get up out my house, man," I demanded.

"Who is this? The new nigga? You the new nigga, my man?" he mocked.

"I'm the *only* nigga. And if you don't back out that door, you'll be the *dead* nigga. Feel me?"

"Oh yeah? Let's see who gets to their piece first. Because you obviously ain't got shit on you, bro," he said, slightly raising his shirt to show a pistol wedged in the waist of his jeans. I mustered up every ounce of strength I had to keep from approaching him with a fist to his face. I don't know who this nigga thought he was but he would not have any dominance over me in my house.

"Okay, Patrick you have to go now! I will not have this in my house. Take your little pistol and get the fuck out. I don't have the patience for you right now," Joya said.

"Cool, *Joy*. But I swear you'll see me again real soon," he said. As he backed out of the house, he blew a kiss to Joya and I stared intently into his dark face. He kept his eyes on me until finally exiting the house. I wasted no time addressing the issue while it was still burning in my mind.

"Explain what the hell that was," I started.

"*That* was Patrick," she replied.

"And?"

"Patrick is an ex,"

"An ex?" I repeated. I was already fuming but her short answers made me crazy.

"Yes, an ex. He always hung around me and tried to do some things that I didn't want to do anymore,"

"Why do I feel like you're not telling me the whole story?"

"Because the whole story doesn't matter. Look, he's no longer a factor, okay? And I'm late for work. I gotta go,"

"If he ain't a factor then why was he in my house, Joya?!"

"Get off your power trip, Jayson. This is still *my* house," she said and walked out the front door. I felt sick to my stomach. It was like my whole body had a pulse and I couldn't breathe. But I was so angry. I couldn't figure out what had just happened. I wanted so badly to chase Joya out the door and tell her where she can put *her* house but my body said no. My legs found a mind of their own and led me to the bathroom where I'd hunched over the toilet and emptied my stomach. The strain on my insides made me feel so vulnerable, like I needed someone to take care of me. But I ignored it. I cupped some water from the bathroom faucet and rinsed my mouth out before staggering to the living room sofa and falling to my back. I closed my eyes and drifted off to a painless sleep.

The house was dim and an orange glare peeked through the curtains as the sun began to set. A silence hung through the air in a way that was unusual for this house. My headache had eased though my stomach was still a bit queasy. I sat up and stretched my neck before getting up and making my way to the kitchen for a glass of water. I sipped slowly, trying to remember what had gone on in the past twenty-four hours. I sauntered up to the second floor bedroom to check the time on my cell phone, noticing I had five missed calls. One was from Jordan while the other four were from my mother. I decided not to call Jordan back since it wasn't important enough for him to leave a message. I quickly dialed my mother's number.

"I'm glad you could take time away from your busy schedule to call me back," she answered.

"I'm sorry, Mama, I was asleep. What's going on?" I apologized.

"Your sister. I don't know where she's at,"

"Okay, well Mama, she's grown. I'm sure she's fine,"

"No, you don't understand. She left last night and I haven't seen her since,"

"What do you mean, you haven't seen her? She didn't tell you where she was going or who she was going with?"

"Does she ever? Look, all I want you to do for me is go look for her," she said. I groaned to myself. This was the last thing I felt like doing. And there was no telling what my sister had gotten into or who she was with.

"I don't know where she would be," I continued.

"Well, find out,"

"That's kind of hard since she doesn't have a phone,"

"Why don't you ask Shawn?"

"Shawn? Why Shawn?"

"She could've spent the night with him. I mean he was all over her last night. You don't remember?"

"No, I don't remember that. But Traycee's not really feeling Shawn like that,"

"That's not how it looked to me. Look, it's worth a shot. Just find my daughter, please,"

"Okay, Mama. I'll try. Love you," I promised and hung up the phone. I sighed deeply and rubbed my face before going to take a shower. I figured that Traycee was just running the streets as usual with her friends trying to remember what it felt like to be free. There was no reason to be alarmed--I was sure--regardless of how my mother felt. After getting dressed and suddenly remembering that I had to go to work later that night, I grabbed my phone from the bed and called Shawn.

"What's good?" he answered.

"Where's my sister?" I started. I didn't feel the need to shoot the shit considering the fact that my patience was so low.

"What?"

"Where's Traycee?" I pretended that the commotion in the background prevented him from fully hearing me.

"Look, she's good. She's safe. Chill out,"

"Bro, if you go out with my sister you need to tell me,"

"Why? She's grown,"

"Because I'm her brother, that's why. Look, just tell me where she is so I can get my Mama off my back. I know you know,"

"She's right here. Hold up," he said. Before long, I heard Traycee's voice on the other end of the phone.

"Hello," she started.

"Traycee, where are you?"

"Clearly, with Shawn,"

"Don't play that shit with me. You don't understand, when you come up missing, I gotta hear it from Mama. Don't ever leave the house and not come back all night unless you tell Mama not to wait up,"

"It's not that big of a deal,"

"It's not? And since when are you fucking with Shawn?"

"Maybe since last night,"

"So you *did* fuck him?"

"Why are you so deep in my business?"

"I wish you would stop being so hot. I hope you used a condom. I know that nigga better than you do,"

"It's not like that,"

"Yeah, okay. Just call Mama and let her know you're okay,"

"Yeah, I will," she said before hanging up the phone. I didn't want to think it. I couldn't fathom having such a thought about my sister, whom I'd kill for. I just kept repeating it over and over again in my head, *my sister is not a ho, my sister is not a ho.* Traycee was always around the opposite sex. And she never kept company with boys her own age. Her type was grown-ass men only with a street lifestyle and a prison mentality. Once I'd gotten caught up with my own drug hustle I hadn't made the time to watch after her like I should've been. Sometimes I blame myself for how she turned out. She was smart and beautiful with the ability to do anything she set her mind to. But she let herself be attracted to the worst kind of man who'd force her to forget that. And it was my job to keep that from her. A job I'd failed. I never understood her fascination.

Even though I trusted Shawn, I couldn't necessarily trust Traycee. I called my mother to make sure that she knew Traycee was okay because I didn't believe that Traycee would do it. She seemed relieved but I could sense some worry still in her voice. I tried to convince her that Shawn was a good guy, at least for the most part, so there was no need to be concerned. But I barely believed my own words. I knew how Shawn was with women and I didn't want my sister to be one of those women. I had already lost one friend and I didn't want to lose another. Traycee was no better. I felt like I had lost control and wasn't sure that I could get it back.

As I rubbed my face, I suddenly remembered what had happened with Joya before I fell asleep. I threatened a man's life for her and she returned that respect by downplaying my role in this house. I wasn't the one on the power trip. I mean, had I become a bum nigga without knowing it? I didn't think so. But maybe that's how Joya saw me. She saw me as someone she had to take care of. Someone who sat around all day and played around all night. I don't think she paid attention to how I left my world as I knew it behind because it looked as though she saw potential in me. How I chose her over everything. And yet she never hesitated to throw her good deeds in my face in every argument we had. To me, she hadn't done that much anyway. So she had some pull in the legal system, big whoop. She allowed me to move in with her after I'd lost my house; but I never would've lost my house if she hadn't talked me into quitting my hustle in the first place. I was beginning to wonder why I had continued this relationship for this long.

My phone rang again. I blew air to the ceiling, hoping that at some point I would have time to rest my mind.

"Yes," I answered irritated.

"Jayson?" the female voice said.

"Yeah, who is this?" I said. I couldn't readily identify her voice and pulled the phone from my ear to see what number read across the display. It was one I didn't recognize.

"Wow, I thought you would've known my voice. But then again, it has been a while,"

"That's great," I said sarcastically. "I still don't know who you are,"

"Sweetheart, it's Jacqui," she said.

"Who?"

"Remember, you sister Traycee introduced us a couple of years ago. We had one really good night before I left for New York the next morning,"

"Oh," I remembered. Jacqui was a sexy motherfucker, even with tattoos covering her thick body. I started to recall the night we had together, full of intimate role play and passionate

111

sex to follow. That was a good night.

"Yeah," she continued. "I know you remember,"

"Yo, what's up? How'd you get my number?" I wondered.

"I have my ways. How are you?"

"I'm cool. Training for football camp this summer,"

"Oh, really? Well, listen, I'm in town and I was wondering if you wanted to get together?" she asked. I thought for a second. I could use the attention of a girl who at least acted like she wanted to be around me. It would give me a break from the chaos that Joya brought and allow me to figure out what I wanted to do about us. Then, I suddenly decided against it.

"You know what? I'm still nursing a hangover so, maybe another time," I told her.

"Are you sure?" she pleaded.

"Yeah, I just can't do it today. Plus, I have to work tonight,"

"Well, okay. I hope you feel better. But don't keep me waiting long,"

"Of course not," I said. I hung up the phone and silently hoped that I hadn't just opened up a can of worms. I didn't want to be that man that cheated on his girl the first chance he got. But that doesn't mean I wasn't tempted. Usually, just thinking of Joya's face would bring me back to reality in a second. However, Joya was stepping in on my bad side. Jacqui wasn't.

I made myself a turkey sandwich before taking a long shower and getting myself ready to go to work that night. After leaving the house, I started off down the street towards the train station. I reached in my pocket for my phone and turned it off. I didn't want to be bothered with anything social. I dropped the phone back into my pocket and looked to the left before crossing the street. I saw Joya standing underneath a streetlight with an unidentified man. She was laughing and flirting with him and I noticed their fingertips were affectionately intertwined. Joya was wearing a short, dark-colored mini-dress and knee-high boots under her winter coat and her hair was washed into natural curls. I strictly remembered that when she left the house her hair was pulled back into a bun and she was wearing a business suit. I quietly watched their conversation until it came to an end about twenty minutes later. The two embraced in a tight hug and kissed like no one was watching. My blood turned hot all of a sudden and I had to go home. I started off in the opposite direction and snatched my phone from my pocket, dialing the last number that was made to my phone.

I called into work and met Jacqui on the other side of town at her hotel. In the elevator towards the fourth floor I thought I would feel my conscience kick in and tell me to go home but it didn't. I knocked twice on the door; no conscience. Jacqui opened the door as if she knew what she had the power to do to me. She wore open a long silk, red robe over a matching, see-through bra and panties. She was rubbing scented lotion in her palms as she invited me into the dimly lit suite. Lit candles were placed all over the room as Aaliyah's voice played softly from a portable sound system. Still no conscience. I sat on the plush sofa, taking in the full ambiance.

"I didn't know if we were going out or staying in so, I just didn't get dressed. You want something to drink?" Jacqui asked.

"Sure, what you got?" I said.

"Red wine. Is that okay?"

"Sure, why not?"

"You know," she continued as she brought me a glass and sat down close to me, "I didn't think you would actually come,"

"Why?"

"Well, word around the street is you have a girl,"

"Oh, that's nothing," I lied as I sipped my drink. "I was surprised to hear from you, though. It's been a while,"

"Yeah, it has. We had a good night that night,"

"Yeah, we did," I smiled. Jacqui leaned in closer to me.

"We can relive old times, I mean, if that's what you want to do,"

"That's cool with me," I obliged. Jacqui climbed on top of me and slowly kissed me. Still no conscience. As I grabbed her warm thighs I could feel my piece pulsate and rise. She gently grinded her cat against my jeans when I pulled the robe from her back and caressed her skin. Jacqui unhooked her bra, which already left very little to the imagination, and dropped it next to us on the couch. I admired her full breasts for a short moment before filling my mouth with the right one. I bit down on her nipple gently and slowly pulled away but dove back in and caressed it with my tongue. I whispered, "Where's the bedroom?" Jacqui pointed in the direction of the room. I picked her up, holding her by her round ass, and carried her to the bedroom. I dropped her on the king-sized bed and immediately removed my shirt, then dropped my pants. Jacqui slid underneath the covers, keeping her eyes on me, and removed her panties. Her eyes quickly shifted down to my bulging crotch and back up again as if to say it was my turn. I stepped out of my forest green boxers and joined her under the covers. I kissed her lips passionately and licked her neck as she spread her legs and reached for protection.

At that moment, I was all ready to jump inside of her and literally take a ride down memory lane. The second the condom hit the top of my shaft, I was halfway into her. I started off as if I was making love to her when I realized I didn't love this girl. In fact, I barely knew this girl. Before I could get attached to her pussy, I turned her over on her stomach and entered her from behind. While on my knees, I pushed her ass fat towards her lower back and pounded her kitty cat until it dripped onto my fingers. Jacqui twisted and turned her head as she screamed for me to go deeper and harder. She cried out my name in satisfaction while I pressed my hands into her torso.

The night repeated its events but in many different ways. Kama sutra played out from the bed to the floor to the couch to the bathtub. I had forgotten about Joya. And while I waited for my conscience to stop me, it never did. It allowed me to bask in my enjoyment of this beautiful woman in front of me. She didn't tell me that I could do better. She didn't remind me of how she sucked my dick without my request and how she deserved to get the same in return. Jacqui was there waiting to give me what she knew I wanted with only the expectation that I do it how I did it before. She appreciated what I gave her and asked for nothing more. It felt good.

By the time I arrived home the next morning as the sun had just risen over a quiet and clear city, I was physically and emotionally drained. I had cheated on Joya and enjoyed it, refusing to feel sorry about not one second. I strut through the front door with my mind on my pillow. I started up the stairs and nearly stepped on Joya's toes as I noticed her sitting at the top. Her head was down until she lifted it slowly and stared a hole into my face. Though I looked her in the eye, I said nothing. I walked around her and went straight to the bedroom. I kicked my shoes off when I heard the door slam close behind me. I turned to face Joya's furious face. She threw her hands up as if to emphasize that she was waiting on an explanation. I stared back at her like I had no clue what she was referring to.

"So, are you going to tell me where you were all night? And I dare you to tell me you were at work, because the club closes at three," Joya started calmly.

"Well, why can't I lie and say I was at work? You do it," I responded.

"What the hell are you talking about?"

"Oh, you don't know what I'm talking about? You got so many niggas that you can't keep them straight?"

"What?"

"I saw you last night with your little boyfriend around ten o'clock, wearing some short-ass dress with those damn boots. Or should I say your *other* boyfriend,"

"Jayson, let me explain..."

"Go ahead, explain. Because I've been *waiting* to see how you get yourself out of this one," I said, crossing my arms and watching her intently.

"Marcus--"

"Oh, Marcus," I interrupted. "So this ain't the same dude who ran up in here yesterday? Go on,"

"Marcus is just a friend I've known for a while. He just got out of jail yesterday so I went to see him," she confessed.

"Really? Just a friend? If that's so then what was up with your ho-dress and the hugs and kisses?" I questioned. Joya buried her head in both hands as I continued, "Are you sure there's nothing going on between y'all?"

"That was nothing,"

"Really? It didn't look like nothing,"

"We dated once and we never officially broke up. But he kissed *me*, I didn't kiss him,"

"Even so, you looked like you liked it. I'm not stupid, Joya. I guess he didn't care that you had a man, but then again why should he? You didn't,"

"I didn't get a chance to tell him,"

"Well, that's funny since the conversation I saw was going on for at least twenty minutes, so I'm pretty sure you had enough time to mention you had a man,"

"Well, Jayson, what do you expect me to do? I'm tired of supporting you. You have to do for yourself because I can't handle it no more," she cried. I felt steam blow out of my nose and ears.

"What the fuck do you think I'm doing?! I was fine until you came along and got in my head. You will not keep throwing that shit in my face. What do you want, a thank you? If that's what you want then, thank you. But fuck you for treating me like I ain't shit to you,"

"Fuck me? No, Jayson, fuck you! If I was gonna cheat on you then I would kick you out but I haven't because I love you and I want to be with you. I'm sorry, okay. I just got weak, and I liked the attention,"

"Yeah, well, I got weak and got a little attention too," I revealed. I didn't think before I spoke but maybe she would realize that I really didn't need her either. Joya wasn't the only one who felt a need to stray.

"What?" she replied, squinting her eyes. "So, you cheated on me? To prove a point?"

"You know, the world doesn't revolve around you, Joya. I

wasn't trying to prove a damn thing to you. But if I did, then it's all good. I'll take that too," I said. Joya gasped at the thought of me being with another woman. She began tearing up when she let out a loud scream and darted toward me in a livid rage. Joya pounded her fists at me repeatedly. I tried to grab her arms and pull them away from me. In the midst of the excitement, her fist bashed the side of my face and before I could think, my own anger took hold and I slammed my fist into her jaw. Her head damn near spun off her shoulders as she stumbled backwards and let out a loud gasp. Joya stared at me with her mouth wide open and the skin around her eye beginning to redden. Tears started to form as she held her face and tried to contain herself. I immediately started to apologize. The last thing I ever wanted to do was hit her. I wasn't that type of man. I never put my hands on a female. But it was almost like I thought she was a man the second her fist hit my face. I just tripped over my own apology as Joya screamed for me to get out. I didn't know what else to say. She clenched her fists together and violently sucked air. I could tell she was on the verge of charging at me again so I just stepped around her and left without words.

I didn't know where to go or what to do. This was not something I'd dealt with before. Usually, I'd go running to my mother for some advice but I couldn't handle her disappointment in me. Going to Traycee was definitely out of the question. Due to the circumstances, she would side with Joya in a heartbeat. I would still be on my own. Counting on my friends for good advice was hit and miss. Sometimes they held responsible answers that made all the sense in the world. Other times, I had to question why I thought them to be a viable source of information in the first place. I guess this was one to keep to myself. I knew I needed to make it right with Joya. But how? What could possibly turn this terrible situation into a good one? I sat on the front porch in the frosted weather unable to think of anything. Suddenly, I began having a thought that reoccurred in my head on a regular basis. It was a large gesture but would show her that I will go out of my way to make her happy. But I didn't know if I really wanted to do this or if I was doing it just so she would forget the fact that I'd actually hit her.

It was now that I had to speak with my mother. I wouldn't tell her that I'd hit Joya, only that I was planning something for her. I knew what my mother would say but at the same time she might help me understand whether or not I wanted this. I should've already known but my mind was so clouded with the image of me punching my girlfriend in the face that I couldn't see anything else. I needed a third party to help me decide.

11

"Mama!" I yelled as I darted through my mother's house. My energy level was incredibly high considering I hadn't slept since two nights before. I still couldn't get the thought of me hitting Joya out of my head and I was afraid that this was the end for us; although, I wondered if that was such a bad thing. I stopped by to speak to my mother this afternoon after running a quick errand and before going to the gym. I had thrown my duffle bag to the side of the front door when I rushed through the house as if someone was dying. I continued screaming for her when Traycee came running from the kitchen.

"Excuse you, rudeness," she started. "Mama is asleep,"

"No, I'm not," Mama said. She was walking from the living room with a grogginess in her voice as she rubbed her eyes.

"What do you want, son?" she continued.

"I need to talk to you. It's important," I told her. I was damn near out of breath. My stamina just wasn't what it used to be.

"Okay, what?"

"It's about Joya,"

"What happened?"

"Traycee, can you leave us alone for a minute?" I asked as I turned and looked at my sister. Her eyes transferred back and forth from my eyes to Mama's.

"I'll find out later anyway so why do I have to leave?" Traycee questioned.

"Traycee?" Mama said.

"Mama?" Traycee whined.

"Traycee, go," Mama demanded. Traycee rolled her eyes and groaned her way upstairs. I stared into my mother's face and felt like I was sweating bullets. She looked back at me with worry lines forming on her face as if I was about to tell her that Joya was in the hospital or something. I kept my hands in my pockets and twirled a small box around in my hand. I couldn't breathe. Why was I so nervous? It was a simple thing for a man like me to admit to his mother. I should've been excited about this. This was way too much for my mind. I couldn't do it. I kissed my mother on the cheek and left.

By the time I had gotten to the gym I thought I would feel better. But I still had the same anxiety I had since Joya and I fought. I ran and ran on the treadmill as if I was literally running from my problems. I could feel my heart rate increase severely until it pounded through my chest. I breathed relentlessly as the sweat covered my body and soaked my gray tank top ten threads at a time. I focused my eyes on the open view of the city of Atlanta in front of me and focused my ears on the heavy metal piercing through my earphones. I always listened to rock music when I worked out. It had the tendency to make me feel its aggressions and motivated me to get them out. It made me work harder. I lifted until my arms were burning, adding more and more weight every time I got bored. I didn't feel like questioning myself any longer. By the time my chest hurt and I could barely breathe, I'd decided to make the jump I was so afraid to make. If I wound up screwing myself then so be it.

I rushed back home like my ass was on fire. The sun was setting and orange footsteps pranced across the sky. I found Joya in the upstairs bedroom changing into a plain white, oversized t-shirt; no pants. She didn't hear me enter the room as she paid close attention to her cell phone. I cleared my throat a little, forcing her to turn abruptly and face me. Joya sighed heavily. I imitated her sentiment before approaching her.

"Before you say anything," I started calmly. "I'm sorry. The last thing I ever intended to do was put my hands on you. With that being said, I have something to ask you,"

"What could you possibly have to ask me?" she wondered. I'd thought about our relationship so far. She cheated on me, I cheated on her; she hit me, I hit her. Although I don't condone this type of thing, I realized that this was us. We might as well get used to it since neither one of us had the balls to leave the other and stay gone. We were stuck to each other worse than the tattoos on Jacqui's body.

"After all this bullshit," I continued, "we both know you're not going anywhere and neither am I. So, why don't we just get married?"

"I'm sorry, what? What the hell are you thinking?" she said. I dropped my gym bag on the bed and rifled through it for the small box. The second I'd found it, I opened it and shoved the two-carat diamond engagement ring in her face. Joya froze. She stared intensely at the ring with a hint of confusion covering her face. Joya was speechless but struggled to respond through halted words. Her reaction amused me. In my experience, women would give into damn near anything at the sight of a proposal. I almost thought her to be a bit spineless but snapped back into the task at hand. While she still fought to speak, I told her not to worry, I would wait. I set the ring in her left hand and started off to the bathroom to take a shower. Upon my return-- and feeling much better, mentally and physically--Joya was sitting at the foot of the bed with her back straight and poised as if she was waiting for me. I stepped in front of her and her eyes nervously moved around the room. Before I could ask what she had decided, she raised her head to watch me, a tear falling from her eye, and held all five fingers up in front of her face to show the ring on her hand. I pulled her up from the bed and embraced her, kissing her on the cheek.

And it was done. It didn't feel like it, but Joya and I were engaged to be married. I already started to wonder, what did I do? I loved her but I was damn near in the mood to break it off with her and go back to the old life that I thought was better. But I had to question if I could live my life without her. Or even if I wanted to. Strangely, Joya consumed my life and I hated it but loved it at the same time. I didn't want to be alone, and as messed up as it seemed, Joya fit me. Likewise, Joya couldn't live without me either. What made me so sure of myself had just played out in front of me. And just like that, I didn't care any- more whether or not it was the right time or how sincere I was. I couldn't take it back now, so I planned to ride this thing until the wheels fell off.

Sliding by my mother's house and telling her was a breeze; in fact, much easier than I thought it would be. Our engagement was something she had been waiting on from the beginning. I watched her squeal with Traycee and Joya while they started to make plans for the wedding. I stood idly by while they ignored me and I wished I had a life outside of these three women. I started to remember Josh mentioning a party going on that night and thought it would be a good getaway from Joya. I slipped out of the house without so much as a goodbye and called Josh to verify the location.

"Oh, your girl is letting you out tonight?" Josh teased.

"Look, nigga, I'm grown. You can bet I'll be there...alone," I assured him. As much as I enjoyed spending time with Joya, I needed to get out by myself. I was still young and I felt like I hadn't had a good night of pure, unadulterated fun in a long time. I could recall the last time I'd been out as just me and my boys, trolling for chicks and being so drunk that we couldn't do anything but laugh at the sickening hangover that followed. I was starting to miss Derek. Even after everything he'd done to me, stealing from me and raping my girl, there was still a place in my heart for him. We had more good times than bad and I wished he was here to be a part of what was going on in my life. We'd always agreed that when one of us got married, the other would be the best man. When one of us had kids, the other would be godfather. But now I felt that whatever choices I made would be a betrayal to him, even though I owed him less than nothing.

Midday had approached and I had been on and off the phone with my mother for most of the day talking about what she wanted for the wedding. The closest thing to a date that had been set was for no longer than a year from now but it didn't make a difference to me at the time. I was itching for a high. Since I had lost all contact with my main connects, I sent Josh a text message and asked him to bring a couple of blunts to the party in a few hours. And I swear that was the roughest two hours and forty-five minutes of my life. By the time I ran into him at the crowded downtown house, I was damn near hanging off his jock for a hit. The two of us sat on the black leather love-seat amongst the group of familiar--and unfamiliar--faces and rolled two blunts worth of the weed from Josh's pocket. I fired it up and sat back, relaxed and nodding my head to the loud music pounding through my ears. I was feeling the effects and was beginning to enjoy myself. I dropped some ash on my teal, collared shirt, and after brushing them past my jeans I headed to the lit kitchen and fixed me a drink of pineapple juice and gin. After taking a few big gulps, I felt an aggressive pat on my back and turned to see Shawn behind me with a wide grin.

"Oh, shit, what's good?" I greeted him with a handshake. I hadn't talked to him for a couple of days, since I'd found out he was sleeping with my sister. I still wasn't too happy about that. But it was good to see him.

"Good to see you out, bro," Shawn said.

"Yeah, yeah. I'm just happy you're not with my sister,"

"Jay," he chuckled. "It's not like that,"

"Yeah, I know exactly what it's like. And I promise, if you do anything to my sister I *will* kill you,"

"Look, there's no need for all that. I'll be real with you. I'm really feeling your sister. Traycee might be rough but I can tell she's a good girl at heart. This ain't just one of my hit-it-and-quit-it moments. I really like her,"

"Really?" I said as I watched Shawn nod his head.

"Yeah, it kind of reminds me of you and Joya. It's real,"

"Real dysfunctional," I scoffed, "speaking of...I fucked up, man,"

"Talk to me,"

"I asked Joya to marry me," I confessed. Shawn's eyes grew wide and his body froze.
"I know you didn't just say what I think you said," he replied. I nodded my head in assurance. "Why would you go and do something stupid like that? You're supposed to be the smart one out of the group,"

"I know, man. I was in a tight spot and I panicked,"

"What did you do?"

"Yo, let's go outside," I suggested. The two of us stepped out into the clear night air where a faint breeze blew across our faces. I looked up into the deep blue sky and started to count the stars. "Basically, what happened is, I caught her cheating on me,"

"Damn,"

"Yeah, some dude she used to date. The nigga just got out of jail so she thought it was cool to go fuck with him,"

"I know you didn't let that slide,"

"Hell no. You remember Jacqui?"

"Jacqui?" Shawn thought. Then, it came to him. "Oh, yeah, I remember you saying something about her a while back,"

"An eye for an eye," I said. I took a hit from the blunt and held the smoke in my lungs for a few seconds as I let Shawn marinate on what I was telling him. I released the smoke slowly before speaking again. "We got into it and I threw that shit right in her face. She didn't know what to say. And when she came at me, I thought she was a dude for a minute and swung back at her,"

"Whoa, so you hit her?"

"I hit her,"

"And *that's* why you asked her to marry you?"

"What else was I supposed to do? I felt bad. I ain't never been a nigga to hit a female. My mama would kill me,"

"Why couldn't you just break up with her?"

"And be a grown man living with my mama? I'm good. Besides, it might make things better,"

"Haven't you learned that marriage makes everything worse? You know what, you dug this whole, you find a way out of it. I'm going back in here to see if I can take somebody home real quick,"

"Excuse me?" I said. If I wasn't mistaken, Shawn had just told me that he had real feelings for Traycee, so I know he wasn't about to go commit suicide and mess with someone else.

"I'm just playing, man. Calm down," Shawn laughed. That's

what I'd thought.

"Yeah, keep playing. That shit will get you killed," I laughed with him and smacked the back of his head as I followed him back into the house.

The party had seemed to be a lot more explosive. Just about everyone was drunk or high, including myself. The music was just right so I grabbed the first beautiful woman I noticed from a dark corner and pulled her close to me for a dance. I leaned against the wall as the brown-skinned beauty swirled her hips at my waist. I felt the warmth of her body with my hand on her bare thigh just below the snug canary yellow dress she struggled to hide her parts with. She swung her brick red hair from left to right while I watched her ass clap in front of me. As she stood back up in her rose-colored Louboutin pumps, I briefly looked over to my right down a dim and narrow hallway leading to the back of the house. I thought I was hallucinating. I wiped my eyes and blinked heavily. I couldn't be that drunk. I didn't even smoke the whole blunt. I had to go. I tapped the girl with no name and swiftly walked outside. I needed fresh air. I needed to get home. Too bad I wasn't a hundred percent sure where I was. I just couldn't remember. My mind was everywhere at once. I just started walking.

About ten minutes later, I recognized the buildings around me and realized that I was walking in the wrong direction. I made a U-turn and headed for the closest train station. I found myself back in front of the very house I had just come from when I heard my name called by a female voice. I jumped, full of paranoia, and walked towards the girl by the front door.

"Why'd you leave?" she asked.

"Because I saw something I couldn't take looking at," I replied.

"Oh, yeah. I'm Precious by the way,"

"Jayson,"

"I noticed you wandering around. Where's your car?"

"I rode here with my boy,"

"Well, if you don't want to go back in there we could hang out at my spot. You look like you need a quiet place to chill out," Precious suggested. I quickly agreed before following Precious to her champagne-colored Hyundai Elantra. The night blurred past me and, before I knew it, I was standing in the middle of the petite living room at her apartment in the ghetto. Precious led me back to her bedroom where I sat on the queen-sized bed, confused. I looked around at the unfamiliar territory and then ran my hand across the black and white bed spread. Precious had left my sight and, when she returned, had slipped out of her body-hugging dress and stood before me in a pale pink bra and panties. What is with these women?, I thought. The moment I noticed her slim body in front of me, she mounted me and began to take my clothes off one piece at a time. I looked up at her round face and bright eyes and saw my fiancé, Joya. At that moment, I wanted nothing more than to make up with her. I felt Joya's body, I felt her breath on my chest and smelled her natural fragrance. I made love to Joya that night, and slept with her under our sheets in our bed.

12

I struggled to open my eyes to a bright and unfamiliar bedroom. My stomach was turning and my head was pounding. I glanced over at a naked woman wrapped up in musty, white bed sheets. Clearly, she wasn't Joya. I sighed deeply in disappointment at myself. Lately, my decisions were more than careless. How was it that Joya and I could get married when we were constantly disrespecting one another? We seriously needed some restraint. I could've sworn that I saw Joya's face last night in the same bed that I'd slept in. But, apparently, that wasn't so. I had to get out of this place. I didn't even know where I was. I just had to go.

I slipped from under the covers, trying to avoid waking the clueless creature beside me as she moved slightly before becoming still again. As I pulled on my clothes, I left silently. The morning sun blinded me and a frost hit me like it knew what I had done. I studied my surroundings, trying to remember where I was and how I was going to get home. I drew a blank. I made a left out of the parking lot and kept straight, in hopes that I would run into some familiar territory. A couple of blocks later, I'd realized that I was closer to home than I thought. However, I was starting to feel as though I really didn't want to be there anymore.

My stomach cringed as I approached the front door and hesitated to go in. Last night's disturbing scene at the party made a clear appearance in my head once more before this morning's realization of what me and Joya's relationship actually was soon took center stage. I now knew what had to be done and there was no turning back. Me and Joya are not what we thought we were. We don't belong together at all. At times, it seems to me that she believes she can still live the single life while she molds me into the perfect man she wants me to be. And sometimes I secretly wish that I didn't have the headache of a woman so strong-minded and careless. Our two worlds clashed in a way where we wanted to be together, but we couldn't.

The door creaked as I slowly entered. I drug my hand across my face as if trying to wipe away the guilt from my sins. I took my walk-of-shame one heavy foot at a time up the stairs and to the bedroom where I'd remember countless hours of talking, arguing and making up after. I stepped toward the bed; a ray of sunlight over Joya's sleeping face. A slight grin came across my face when I got on my knees and quietly asked God to give me the right words to say and the strength to leave her to live her life. I ran my fingers up the length of her arm and gripped her shoulder, gently shaking her awake. It was like the first time looking into her eyes; I could almost see her soul. In that one glare I could see the goodness of her heart but the struggle she had giving into the temptations of her mind. I knew that struggle all too well on my own.

She stared at me, as if waiting for me to express the first thought of the conversation.

"I need to talk to you," I began. Joya stayed silent but engaged herself. "We can't do this anymore." Her face seemed to tense up in confusion.

"What are you talking about?" she asked.

"I saw you and Marcus at the party last night, together. We can't keep doing this to each other,"

"Doing what?" Joya questioned. She rose herself with one arm and peered down at me.

"I know you've been cheating on me with that dude. I can't say that you don't care, but I can say that you still do it. And I'm not saying I'm the perfect man because, if I was, I wouldn't have even brought this up. As long as we stay together, we're just gonna keep disrespecting each other. And I love you enough to just let go," I explained.

"Are you breaking up with me?"

"I'm setting you free. It's obvious you're not happy with me and every time I get mad at you I go out and do something stupid. What kind of marriage would that be? We can't live like that,"

"So, after everything we've been through, you're just done? Just like that?"

"Joy, it's not that I don't want to be with you, it's that I can't. And you can't be with me either. The two of us are just not fit to be in a relationship with each other. If we were, there wouldn't be so many people getting in between us,"

"Fine," she said, nodding her head and biting her bottom lip. She was fighting back tears and losing the battle. "You don't love me no more, then I don't love you. Get out."

Joya snatched her ring from her finger and threw it past me before turning to the opposite side and shoving herself under the covers. I rose to my feet and started to pack some things to take with me but thought it best to come back when she wasn't there. I left the house but sat on the porch step, resting my head on my cupped hands. I felt bad. The last thing I wanted to do was hurt her. In fact, I didn't realize she would take it so hard. No, she didn't scream or hit me but the look on her quivering face showed just how quick her heart shattered.

I didn't know where to go at that point. I didn't know who to talk to, or even if I wanted to talk to anyone. I thought I needed to be alone. I changed into a gray tank top and black sweatpants, grabbed my iPhone and headed for the gym. There was a need for an escape away from the world like no other. I drowned out the rhythmic pounding of my feet on the treadmill with the mellow sounds of Frank Ocean as sweat ran down my moistening chest in complete meditation. I kept my eyes straight ahead, staring out of the large wall-to-wall window overlooking the city.

I felt like I was running away to nowhere. The low clouds were like a dream sequence to an unknown destination. To me, I was running through them with no intentions on looking back; I was too afraid I would see Joya following closely behind. At the end of all this, I really didn't want to see her again. I thought if I didn't see her face, it would be much easier to move on.

I needed to keep busy. Working out only cleared my mind for a little while before I thought of Joya again. Every other song reminded me of her, and I had to keep telling myself that it just wouldn't work. What I needed was a day job; something that would keep me occupied until I had to clock in at the club at night. Currently, I had entirely too much time on my hands during the day, which only added fuel to the fire. I couldn't imagine what kind of job I could get considering the fact that it took so long to get the one I had. Either way, it was about that time to get my money up and Joya out of my head.

I waited to catch my breath before I left the gym and thought about where I was going to go. My mother, my friends were all out of the question because I didn't feel like explaining myself. I didn't want to hear from my mother how I needed to talk to Joya. I didn't care if Traycee thought I had messed up. And I for damn sure didn't want to hear any of my friends dog me about how I should be a man and not be so depressed about a woman. Because of this, I still had nowhere to go.

As I left through the front doors of the gym and started off towards the train station, I noticed the hotel on the corner and figured it was a lot better than a park bench. I quickly paid for a room, not knowing exactly how long I would be there. The moment I tossed the key on the nightstand, I pulled my shirt over my head and lied back on the bed. I stared at the display on my phone for a minute and then held down the power button, turning it off. With the curtains closed, the dimly lit room mimicked my melancholy feelings. The sadness drew me in as I covered my eyes with one arm and slept.

For three days I had spoken to no one socially. Little by little I had taken my things from Joya's house while she was away, and only went to work so that I could spend my check on more nights at the hotel. My phone stayed off from the moment I'd pressed the button the day I checked in; there was no one worth talking to until I decided to look for a second job. However, it was getting harder to ignore my friends seeing as how their hangout was Club 112; and I knew my mother may have been starting to worry since the last time she'd heard from me was when Joya and I had announced our engagement. So much for fixing everything.

I was so bored watching reruns and refusing to spend money on Pay-Per-View that I couldn't ignore the urge to get my phone. I was curious to see if anybody had tried to get a hold of me and if anything new was going on with anyone. Once in my hand, I hit the power button and waited for the phone to turn on. After a few seconds, a text message came in; then another and another. I had a total of forty text messages and thirty-two voicemails. My missed calls never showed unless my phone was on when the call came in, but I'm sure there were twice as many calls as there were voicemails. Because it was easier, I went ahead and started on the text messages. Most of them were from my boys wondering where I was and why no one had heard from me. A few were from Traycee, but only one caught my attention. It read:

> "Jayson, I know we didn't end on the best of terms but your mom asked me to try and find you because nobody knows where you are. That makes me worry about you. You don't have to tell me where you are, just let me know you're okay."

My heart stopped. I didn't know what I should do. Should I respond? Should I call her? Joya hadn't left my mind since the last time I had saw her and I did miss her. I just thought it was best for the both of us to stay away from each other; even if it did kill me. I swallowed hard and took a deep breath. My finger floated over her name and all I had to do was tap it once to display the number and once more to call. But did I have it in me to open up that box and see what between us was left? I swallowed again, and my pride went down with it.

This was a mistake, I thought. Why did I do that? I could've just texted her back, or not said anything at all. Yeah, ignoring her is better than anything.

"Jayson?" she answered. *Too late, but I could still hang up.*

"Jayson, I can hear you breathing," she continued. *Damn.*

"Uh...yeah. What's up? You called?" I hesitated, not really sure how to even approach the conversation.

"Yeah, everybody's calling me trying to figure out where you are and I didn't know what to tell them," she said.

"What *did* you tell them?" I asked, fumbling with the folds in my jeans.

"I told them I didn't know. And of course they asked me how I didn't know,"

"And?"

"Well, I said I just didn't know, except for when your mom asked me. I couldn't lie to her. It didn't feel right,"

"So, you told her we broke up?"

"I had to. What else was I gonna tell her? But I guess I'll just let her know that you're okay. You *are* okay, right?"

"I guess," I sighed lowly. "I'm as okay as I can be,"

"Where are you?"

"I can't tell you,"

"Why not?"

"Because you don't need to know. You don't need to be around me. I probably shouldn't have even called you,"

"Jayson, I miss you, for real. Ever since you left I've had time to think about how our whole relationship went down. I never thought I could ever be that type of woman,"

"Me neither. I didn't realize that ol' boy at the party the other night meant more to you than I did,"

"Okay, I deserve that. We both had our moments of disrespecting the other. I just wish there was a way for us to move past it. Even if we don't get back together I at least want to know that you forgive me,"

"I love you too much to hold grudges, Joy. That's why I left. I felt like you would do better without me,"

"But I'm not. Believe it or not, my life sucks without you. As mad as I get, I don't ever want you to leave. Just so long as we both agreed that we would take our relationship seriously instead of acting as though we didn't really care what happened to us,"

"So, you want to be with me?"

"Of course I do. After I spent the night with Marcus that night, I felt so dirty. I felt like a whore and like I didn't even deserve you. Being with him didn't even feel right. It felt like I was just doing it to get back at you for cheating on me. That's not anything that I would do. And then when I woke up the next morning and looked at him, it didn't even feel like it was worth it. All I could see was your face," Joya confessed. Funny, how in-tuned we were with one another. How was it that we were so good but so bad for each other at the same damn time? Either way, I still didn't know if it was worth going back to. How did I know that we wouldn't fall back into the same bullshit we just left; even if we were trying to make it better? This sucked.

"Joya, I don't know if we can do it. Every time we try to start over we do the same shit to each other. Who wants to live their life like that? I know I don't, and I know you don't either," I said.

"So, what do we do?" she asked.

"Be friends? Jumping back into a relationship wouldn't do us any good right now because we need to gain each other's trust back,"

"How did you become so smart?" she said; I could hear the smile in her voice.

"I don't know. Maybe it was when I met this girl a while back who taught me a lot,"

"I don't think she taught you that much,"

"You'd be surprised," I paused. "I love you, Joya,"

"I love you too, Jayson," she replied.

Packing was bad, but unpacking made me want to scream. Where did all this stuff come from? I couldn't even remember using some of it. Trash.

It was my first day in my new apartment and Joya was helping me get settled. It was nothing much, but it was mine. I could finally afford my own place after quitting my job at the club the moment I got the call to work nine hours a day installing, fixing, and maintaining household appliances for Whirlpool. It sure beat the hell out of playing videogames all day until I went to work, only to deal with drunk fools who never tipped. I was happy in my new environment and about the significant pay raise I received. It was about time I was able to get my own ride instead of living on the train. I didn't get back my Caddy because I couldn't really see myself in one anymore; so I settled on a smaller Impala.

Joya and I were finally on the same page. We were taking it slow, just enjoying each other's company. We practiced being honest and comfortable, and focused on finding a friendship before we found love again. Even though I constantly wanted to jump her bones, I resisted. I knew sex could only lead to struggle and confusion and I was *just* getting my life to a point that I could stand it. I wanted to focus on what we were building.

"Jay," Joya began. "I swear you have more shoes than me,"

"I doubt it," I laughed.

"What do you want me to do with these empty boxes?"

"Just throw them out of the way somewhere and I'll get them later," I told her. As we scuffled through the mess that was my living room, there was a faint knock at the door. I scurried over to answer. As I opened the door, Traycee jumped into my arms and kissed me on the cheek. She hugged Joya as Shawn walked in quietly behind her, greeting me in the process. The two looked around with pride and acceptance while joyfulness filled the room.

Traycee and Shawn had been together seriously for almost six months and it had been a while since I'd seen her so happy. I had noticed actual changes in Shawn and how much he genuinely loved my sister. I never thought I would be down for this relationship, knowing the two of them so well and how bad they were at relationships. But who was I to judge?

"What are y'all doing here? I wasn't gonna have anybody

over here until I got everything straight," I wondered.

"Well," Traycee started, "we have something to tell you." She was so bubbly and happy I could only think that maybe they were about to announce their engagement. They haven't been together *that* long though.

"Traycee, will you calm down and let the man get settled in his new place first? You can wait for a better time," Shawn pleaded.

"Oh, come on. He's my brother. Why can't we tell him now?" she begged, holding on to his hands and giving him her best puppy-dog look. I smiled in amusement; and a little bit of excitement.

"Okay, fine. I don't know why I fall for that look every time. Go on and tell him," Shawn surrendered. I crossed my arms at my sister.

"I'm pregnant," she whispered happily. My stomach hit the floor and no words would leave my mouth. All I could hear was Joya squealing while my body was paralyzed. I had to ask myself if this was real. My baby sister was not only a grown woman but she was about to become a mother. A year ago I would have been ready to kill both of them, but I was happy to have a little niece or nephew on the way. We needed a miracle in our family.

"Well, bro, you were already like family anyway. Now it's official," I said to Shawn as I welcomed him as my real brother. I turned around and hugged Traycee tightly as if to tell her that I was glad she was giving us such a gift.

"How pregnant are you?" I asked.

"About seven weeks," she answered.

"Oh, wow," I awed, smiling and holding her stomach in amazement. "Does Mama know?"

"Yeah, and she's happy. You know how bad she wants a grandkid,"

"Yeah," I nodded.

"I'm so glad you're not mad at me,"

"Well, a baby is a blessing and I can't be mad at you for bringing us a blessing. You're responsible, and both of y'all mean a lot to me so I can't wait for this kid to get here," I assured her. Tray-cee jumped into my arms again.

Just like that, it seemed as if my life was taking a sharp U-turn for the better. Joya and I were on good terms and Traycee was out of prison and about to have a baby with one of my best friends; not to mention my finances were on point without me having to sell dope. I liked this honesty thing. Things couldn't get any better.

13

I took a swig of ice cold water and wiped the sweat from my forehead before taking off towards the 75-yard line. This isn't exactly what a man should be doing on New Year's Eve at 11PM but I have to train. The stadium lights at the Georgia Dome blared down on the cold, wet grass as I shuffled up and down the field with my boys Jordan and Josh. Just as I was about to tell Josh to go long for another drill, he stopped me.

"Aye hold up, man!" he yelled, waving his hand and approaching me. He was clearly out of breath with sweat dripping from his face. He bent over and continued, "Dude...we've been...oh my God...we've been out here for four hours." Josh kneeled to the ground, still heaving and trying to catch his breath.

"Damn, shawty, you running out of steam already?" I laughed.

"Fuck...you mean...*already*?" he said as if he was offended. He rose from the ground.

"My nigga, I ain't played since high school; and you got me out here like I'm in the league and shit,"

"I hate to say it but he's right," Jordan interrupted. "You've been back at it for a grip. And we smoke too much for this shit,"

"Man, I thought y'all were my boys, and now you're quitting on me?" I questioned.

"We *are* your boys and we always got your back. But my dude, it's New Year's Eve and I need to be drunk and up under my woman right now,"

"Please," I scoffed, squeezing the football in between both hands. "We all know you ain't got no woman,"

"No sir, the tables have turned. I'm the one getting cutty every night and you, my friend, are getting *nothing* every night. But for real, though, if I don't get back Tangie's gonna kill me for leaving her by herself with that baby all night. And you know how she is,"

"Why would I know how she is?" I thought; and then it dawned on me. "Dude, please tell me you are not dating my cousin?"

"I thought you knew that?"

"Small fucking world," I mumbled. "And that baby is yours?"

"Yeah, dude. I don't claim kids that ain't mine!"

"How old is it?"

"He's six months. Damn, I thought for sure she told you. My bad, bro,"

"I haven't talked to Tangie in at least a couple of years. I ain't even seen her around nowhere. Shit, with everything going on with me and Joya I haven't had the time to focus on anything else,"

"Damn, now I feel like I owe you,"

"Not really. You still gotta deal with Tangie every day. That's enough for me. Get the fuck out of here, man," I joked. I shook his sweaty hand and patted Josh on the back as he chugged water.

"Yo Josh, you sure you don't wanna stay for a couple more minutes?" I mocked.

"Fuck you, Jay," he said. I snickered a little more before grabbing my gym bag from the sidelines and heading out behind them. As I walked through the gate, Joya was standing against her car with her arms crossed. She gave me a sweet smile when she nervously scratched her head through the back of her tousled curly hair. She placed her hands in her coat pocket before she spoke.

"Late practice, huh?" she began.

"How'd you know I was here?" I wondered.

"Your sister told me when I left her little New Year's Eve party,"

"She's having a party?" I quizzed. Traycee was about five months pregnant now and I wasn't comfortable with her being in that type of atmosphere in her condition. I for damn sure didn't want her to be drinking.

"Chill out, it's just an innocent get together. Your mom's there and we made sure she didn't even try to *sneak* a drink. She's good. As a matter of fact, she wanted me to come get you and drag you back there," Joya continued.

"Oh yeah? Well, I don't think I really want to be around a whole lot of people. I've been practicing for a while and I just want to jump in the shower and chill,"

"Okay, since you don't want to be around a lot of people, how about just being around me?" she suggested. I smiled with some slight embarrassment. It was cute that she wanted to spend her New Years with me, being that we had grown into best friends. At the same time, I wasn't sure how I would react being alone with her. It had been months since we'd had sex; eight months, three weeks, and four days to be exact. I was afraid that I was going to go there. Man, did I want to go there. She was so beautiful to me. I said a little prayer in my head and told her to follow me home before getting in my car.

The moment we entered my apartment, I told Joya to make herself at home while I took a quick shower. I heard the television turn on in the living room and someone start talking about Time Square. As the time drew near to midnight, Joya yelled for me to hurry up.

"You're missing it!" she screamed, banging on the bathroom door.

"Alright, I'm coming, I'm coming!" I assured her. The second I turned off the water, I grabbed a towel and threw it around my waist, almost slipping on the wet floor as I rushed out the door. They were counting down as the ball dropped.

5...4...3...2...1...Happy New Year!

I smiled and turned around to embrace Joya with one hand still on the towel. She ran her hands slowly down my back as the left-over water beads ran across her fingertips. Her body was warm. Just then I felt her fingers at the small of my back and my heart began to pound throughout my body. She gazed into my eyes and I could sense the heat emanating from hers. Our lips moved slowly, yet rushed to one another. Joya's hands gripped tightly to my biceps in a failed attempt to contain her emotions.

That kiss, being the first kiss we'd shared since ending our relationship, was sweet. It was innocent; different from any other kiss between us. It was more genuine, in fact, to the point that all I wanted to do was love her. But how was I to end everything we had been working so hard to build? I suddenly pulled away from her.

"You sure about this?" I questioned.

"No," she answered.

"Me neither," I said. I glared down at her round lips and couldn't stop myself. The feeling was too great at this point. I lifted her straight in the air from around her waist and headed for my bedroom. I could feel my bath towel start to loosen and fall from behind. With one knee on the bed, I gently placed her down and lay between her thighs. I wanted to treat her body as if it were a fragile package, acting as if the first sign of mistreatment would force it to fall apart. Removing her clothes one article at a time—first shoes, then shirt, pants, and underwear—I caressed her soft thigh with one hand while kissing her favorite spot on her neck.

As I teased her by massaging her cat with my tense manhood, I felt her wetness signal her readiness. Once I entered her body, Joya gasped and grabbed the back of my neck. I stroked her as slowly and as gently as our first kiss. I wanted her to feel the love and respect I had for her and her body. I didn't want to hurt her. I just wanted her to be satisfied. At that moment, in the midst of Joya's quiet whispers, there was a clarity that came over me. I didn't know if it was just the sex that I missed or if God was trying to tell me something. Either way I was open.

I awoke with a sense of happiness. The brightness of the sun filled the room and kissed Joya's face in a way that made her glow. She lay bundled up under the covers in a peaceful sleep. I positioned myself to face her, examining her features. Her hair was unkempt and tangled while her makeup was faded and smudged, but it was the mark of a good night.

Just as I was about to touch her, my phone began to ring from inside my pants pocket on the floor. I didn't want it to wake Joya so I jumped up, still naked, and grabbed it, hitting the button as fast as I could. I missed the call anyway. Checking the log, it was my mother. I told myself I would call her back later as I focused on programming the phone to vibrate.

"Don't people usually sleep in on New Year's day?" Joya asked groggily from behind me. I turned and noticed she was on her knees but wrapped up in the black blanket.

"Nice ass," she continued. "It's a little tighter than I remember. I guess those drills are paying off,"

"I'm sorry," I began, holding up the phone. "I was trying to turn it off so it wouldn't wake you,"

"It's okay," she said before my phone rang again. "Damn, somebody must really want to talk to you right now,"

"It's just my mama. She probably just wants to tell me Happy New Year. I'll call her back later,"

"Why not just talk to her now?"

"Because I have something more important to talk to you about,"

"Oh, really? Like?"

"Well..." I hesitated. My phone rang again. Damn, Mama! The minute I get some time, you want to jump in the middle. "Happy New Year, Mama,"

"Jayson," she struggled. There were tears in her voice and she could barely speak.

"Mama, are you crying?" I asked, confused. Joya sat on her heels and stared at me in concern. I started to put my clothes on as I waited for her answer me.

"Jayson, something...happened," she continued.

"What happened, Ma?!"

"Traycee...and Shawn..." she sniffled through her words. It was killing me. It was like she wasn't talking fast enough and I didn't know what she was about to say.

"Mama, tell me what happened," I demanded. She took a

141

deep breath.

"Traycee and Shawn got into a car accident last night," she confessed. My stomach dropped. At the same time, I knew they had to be okay. My mama was known for blowing things out of proportion and I know Shawn would be more careful with Traycee knowing that she was pregnant. I just had to get her to stop crying long enough to tell me what hospital they were at. I sat at the edge of the bed.

"Mama, calm down. I'm sure it's not that bad. What hospital did they go to?" I said.

"Jayson...they didn't make it," she cried again. And then my heart dropped into my stomach. I paused, unable to move by my own free will. I breathed short, shallow breaths as the phone slid gently from the side of my face and hit the floor. I was dreaming. I couldn't be awake because this was too horrible to be reality. No, no it was just a really bad nightmare and I was going to wake up soon. I had to wake up soon. Because if I didn't wake up then I wanted to go to sleep and never wake up again. I lowered my head between my legs and aggressively rubbed both palms back and forth over my head. My chest hurt from how hard my heart was beating, and my face hurt from the tears that wanted to come out but wouldn't. How does a man go from the perfect night to the worst fucking morning?

"Jayson. Jayson!" Joya screamed. Her voice faded into my ears because, for a second, I went deaf. After hearing that my only sister and another one of my best friends were dead, nothing else seemed worth hearing.

"Jayson, talk to me! What did she say?" Joya continued. She had left the bed and bent down on the floor in front of me, placing her hands on top of mine which were still on my head. I lifted my head to face her.

"My—my sister...and Shawn," I struggled. I tried to clear my throat as I was so upset I could barely get the words out. "They were in a car wreck. They died,"

"Oh, God," Joya sobbed. She held me tightly and I began to cry into her bare chest. What was I going to do without my baby sister? I had already lost her to prison and the minute I got her back, she was taken from me again. And what about her baby? She was so excited about it; so ready to be a mother. I could tell Shawn loved her. This shit didn't make any sense. How the hell does this happen?

It's like my mind was in overdrive. I knew I needed to be with my mama since I was all she had now. At the same time, I couldn't function. I couldn't remember how to drive. I couldn't even figure out how to get up off the bed and start walking to the front door. I felt useless. I felt like God just took a piece of my heart and crushed it in front of my face. I didn't want to live anymore; not without my baby sister.

As she sat on my lap, I squeezed Joya so hard I thought I might have been hurting her, but she just squeezed me back just as tightly until my tears stopped. After several minutes, I finally got up enough strength to get in my car; however, Joya chose to drive. I probably would have driven into a building anyway. The whole ride, I just stared out of the window. I could only see Traycee's face reflecting back at me. The moment I saw my mother's house my stomach began to hurt. If I was this much of a wreck, I could only imagine what she was feeling.

The second I saw my mother she leapt into my arms and held me tight. She sobbed deeply into my chest as I squeezed my eyes shut, trying to keep more tears from falling. By that time I couldn't see past them. She just cried over and over again, "My baby's gone, my baby's gone!" I tried to tell her it would be alright, but I wasn't sure that it would. After this, I didn't even want to try to be happy anymore. To be real, the only thing that would make me happy would be to no longer live this life. But I couldn't leave my mama. Not right now.

While my mother stood on one side of me, Joya stood on the other and I held their hands tightly as we slowly walked down the aisle of the large, dimly-lit church. We were in the head of the line to view the bodies as they lay peacefully in each casket. My stomach was in knots and I felt myself pulling back. I started to breathe heavily, taking another step forward, and then another until Shawn was in front of me. I was waiting on him to open his eyes and ask me what I was staring at. I kissed my fingers and touched his hands before moving to Traycee. She was beautiful physically but she had lost her glow. I noticed how flat her stomach was. While her hands were cupped at her chest, I placed my palm over them and ran it down the middle of her body to her abdomen. My mother had just kissed her cheek before realizing what I was doing. Before I pulled her away she broke down and moaned over Traycee's body. Joya sadly covered her mouth as we grabbed her from both sides and moved her to her seat on the front bench.

Soon the rest of the church was filled of crying faces in black attire. People constantly hugged and kissed us as they passed with condolences up until the minister took his place at the altar. I'd almost tuned out the entire ceremony until I heard my name. I was called to say a few words on behalf of Traycee and Shawn, yet I had prepared nothing. I'd spent two weeks alone with a pen and paper unable to come up with anything to express my feelings about them. And the last thing I wanted to do was embarrass them by choking. As I got up, Joya yanked my hand; and as I looked back at her, she placed her other hand on her heart and nodded her head. Without words I knew exactly what she meant.

I approached the altar and took the microphone while wiping my eyes semi-dry. I took a deep breath and blew out before speaking.

"You know, this is really hard for me," I started. "Seeing, not only my sister but, one of my closest friends gone. What's funny is that I never saw them together until I saw how happy they were. And it saddens me even more to know that I'll never get to see my niece or nephew. I was looking forward to that. But I've been really selfish. I keep thinking about how losing the two of them affected me, about why people keep getting taken away from *me*. You know, Traycee and Shawn both had hard lives, and it wasn't until a minute ago that I realized how glad I am that they don't have to live hard anymore. My mother always reminded me that God has his reasons for everything, even if we don't understand them. So if they had to go, at least all *three* of them went together."

I turned to face both caskets to tell them I loved them before sitting back down. Joya kissed my cheek and my mother patted me on the back. My mind went over what I had just said. I really *was* being selfish. It was always my life that was going to Hell even if I was the cause. What I needed to start doing was trying to make happy the people I love that are still living and loving me. I vowed right then and there that I would devote my life to making somebody else's meaningful.

It was then my mother rose from her seat and took the microphone. She struggled to speak through her tears but blotted her eyes with tissue and continued.

"My daughter was always a free spirit. She took after her brother on a lot of things but I know he would always look after her. When she went to prison, I never thought I'd see her again. Then one day she called me and told me that she was getting out, and I said, "Traycee, how is that possible? You've only been in there a few years." And she said, "Well, Mama, Shawn pulled some strings for me and got me out so I'll be home tomorrow. I don't know how he did it but I love him even more now." I about broke down in tears." she said. I remembered being so happy that she was out but so confused at how.

"I didn't know who she was talking about," she continued. "And she said Jayson's friend. She said, "He came to see me and we've been talking for a while now." Then she told me how much she cared about him and how much he cared about her. I was so happy when I saw her, and so happy to know that she had someone who I already considered a part of our family; and just like that they were starting their own family. I was ready— I think we were all ready—for her life to change in such a way. I love her. I love the both of them and I hope they knew that I was so proud of them."

It made me smile. If I ever had any doubt about Shawn's feelings for my sister they were crushed in that moment. Knowing that he had cared so much about her drew me even closer to him, and I hoped that in some way he could know how much that meant to me.

That night I prayed. I prayed God would help me understand why they had to go, and that they knew how much I loved them. I didn't want Traycee to die without knowing that I was proud of her. And it was in that *Amen* that I realized how tightly I had to hold on to the people I loved. I didn't have any more time to waste. I had a decision to make and I had to make it now.

14

I hesitated but knocked on Joya's door anyway. I hadn't lived there in so long that I'd forgotten I still had a key. As I was about to look for it in my pocket, Joya opened the door hastily like she was happy to see me and eager to pull me inside. She was wearing a blue, silk bathrobe and her hair was curly and completely wet. I jumped inside as to not let too much of the cold air get in then gently hugged her.

"Hey, you okay?" she began.

"Yeah, yeah I'm good. I mean, it still hasn't really hit me yet," I replied.

"Well, it's only been a couple of days since the funeral. What did you want to talk to me about?"

"Well," I started, placing my hands in my coat pockets. It was now or never. "With Shawn and Traycee's deaths, I realized that I can't wait no more." Joya looked at me confused when she crossed her arms.

"Can't wait no more for what?" she questioned.

"You mean a lot to me. I feel like we've been through the trenches and back, and I still love you. I always have even when I didn't want to. And if you love me, then I think we should be together,"

"So, you want to get back together? I thought we were going to take it slow,"

"I don't have time for slow,"

"Jayson," she held her hands up in front of me. "You're just vulnerable right now. I would be too if I was in your spot. Your mind is just foggy and you need somebody to hold onto right now,"

"My mind has never been so clear. I can learn to accept the fact that they're gone. I did it with Derek. Did I want to? Hell no, but I did and I'll do it again. What I can't accept is the two of us going through life not seeing what's right in front of us,"

"And what's in front of us?"

"Me...and you. Do you still love me, Joya?"

"More than anything. It kills me every day that I see you and at the end of the day I go my way and you go yours. You're my best friend," Joya confessed as she took my face in both hands and her eyes misted. I grabbed both of her wrists.

"Marry me," I said. A tear dropped from each eye when she whispered, "Okay." That's all I needed to hear to grab her and kiss her as if I'd never see her again. She cried into my shoulder and my hands gripped her sides and clenched her robe. It was then that I was more determined than ever to see this through. And to make sure nothing got in the way, I was going to make sure it happened sooner than later.

"Get dressed, let's go," I told Joya.

"Wait, where are we going?" she asked.

"I want us to do this now before I find a way to fuck this up. If we go to the courthouse it'll be done. I don't need the big wedding anyway. All I need is you and I'm good,"

"But I always wanted a wedding. If we get lucky with a venue then we'll be married by the end of the year. It won't take as long as you think,"

"I told you, I don't have time for all that. Okay, look..." I paused. I felt like I was thinking only about myself again. I wanted her to be happy. I didn't want to crush her dreams. "How about we go to the courthouse now and have the wedding later? We don't have to tell anybody that we're already married. I just want to be with you,"

"Okay, I think I can handle that," she agreed. I followed her upstairs to her bedroom and watched as she rifled through her drawers for something to wear, and applied a handful of products to her hair just for it to look about the same as it did when it was wet. I found myself sure but with butterflies in my stomach the closer we got to the petite office-like room to stand in front of the judge. It was happening.

"Do you have any rings for each other?" the man said while he waited patiently for an answer. Joya's face went blank as she started to say no, when I pulled from my pocket the very diamond ring I had given her not even a year before, which was accompanied by a sterling silver wedding band for me. Showing my commitment to only her was just that important to me.

"I got that covered," I smiled. Joya gasped in disbelief as I placed the ring on her hand and she placed mine. It was really happening. I finally kissed her as a husband and felt in no way I had felt before. I was content. I almost felt accomplished, finally finding a woman that was so good for me that she deserved my commitment. This is happiness.

I promised Joya a wedding and that's what I was going to give her. She had planned a ceremony in less than six months and all I had to do was get through the night to marry her all over again. Simple enough. My boys decided to give me a bachelor party considering they didn't know I was already married and they wanted an excuse to relive "The Hangover". I let them do it since I didn't mind having a night like we used to back in the day.

Magic City Gentlemen's Club was packed from wall to wall. I could hear low murmurs underneath the bass-blaring music that bounced around each corner of the room. The large group of us moved to a secluded VIP area and immediately started with shots of liquor. Without realizing it, I was knocking back more and more until my vision was fuzzy. The room was so dark that the only way I knew I was still conscious was by the neon lights that flashed my way every few seconds. I felt the presence of a woman whose face I could no longer recognize; all I noticed was her ass sashay from left to right as she led me somewhere outside of my current location. The air was thick while I stumbled to an unknown destination.

Then everything went black. I woke up by the sun blinding me within a hotel room I had never seen before. My body was sore and swimming in musty, silk sheets. I looked around me as I tried to get up and noticed a woman in the bed next to me, turned on her side and facing the other direction. *Are you kidding me? How could I let myself get that drunk?* I just couldn't believe it. I stepped quietly, as to not wake up this woman and get out without an awkward altercation.

The second I found my clothes, I started out the door and paused. Something told me not to leave until I made sure of something. I scurried across the room, in and under the bed and around every corner. The only thing I found was more regret when I saw the girl's face. And I wanted to kill myself. I left the room with an intense migraine—finding that I was currently in a Howard Johnson's—and took the train across town back home.

I dropped down on my couch and rubbed my head, trying to figure out what the hell I did the night before. I guess I knew what I did, but what I didn't know was why. I took my phone from my pocket and plugged in the dead battery. It was 11AM and I had missed call after missed call and a barrage of text messages. As I read a text from Joya, I screamed, "Oh, shit!" It felt like I was getting dumber by the second. Now I had to hurry and wash the infidelity off of me and get into my tux before noon.

I struggled to button my jacket while I rushed into the church frantically, trying to figure out where I needed to be. Josh grabbed me by the shoulders the second the doors closed behind me.

"Dude!" he said. "Where the hell have you been, man?! These chicks have been going crazy trying to find you,"

"I know, I know. Let's just get started, alright," I huffed. While Josh ran to tell Joya that I had arrived, I walked casually into the sanctuary towards the altar. The pianist began to play and I glanced around at an overly decorated room filled with quietly murmuring people. As I stood next to the pastor, I took a deep breath, hoping to forget what I had just woken up to. At the same time, I was trying to remember how I ended up in the same bed as Diamond. I wasn't depressed. I wasn't upset with Joya; in fact, we were doing so much better than we had in the past. We were in love again. She was my wife now. What the hell was I going through?

By the time I had snapped out of my regretful haze, the doors at the opposite end of the church opened dramatically and I saw an angel emerge from the bright light. Time seemed to stop and all other faces disappeared as Joya moved slowly down the aisle with her curvy silhouette and a long veil covering her face. When I was able to uncover her and stare into her bright eyes, I choked on my vows and fought with my emotions. My guilt and my love for her swirled around each other, and I worked on expressing my commitment over my betrayal.

"Joya," I started, clearing my throat. "I've never been blessed enough to come across a woman like you. You've been my rock even when you've been my problem. Your concern for me brings me to love you like no one else I have ever known. Even in my sister's death, you gave me life. You've become my best friend and I promise that I won't hurt you." These were strong words but I didn't feel like I could do any worse from now on. Sleeping with Diamond was the mother of all mistakes but if I had to walk on eggshells around myself then that was fine with me. I owed it to Joya and to our marriage.

"Jayson, my Jayson," she grinned. "You're right, I *am* your best friend, and you're mine. Everybody may think they know exactly who you are. But they don't. I've seen you, the real you. You're intelligent and ambitious and goofy and loveable...and everything that I've ever wanted. All I ever wanted for you is happiness. And I'm glad you let me be happy with you."
I bit my lip and held her hands tightly. Tears flooded my face. I couldn't believe I was losing my composure so badly. I felt like I used to be a gangsta before Joya came along. A nigga didn't cry unless absolutely necessary; and the only time it seemed to be necessary was at a funeral. I almost felt like I was being a bitch. But I was happy. I loved that girl too much to hide how much she meant to me. Call me a punk if you want to.

When I accepted her hand and kissed her, I remembered New Year's Day when I had kissed for the first time in months and how different it felt. Now this time was that much more different because it was eternal. I kissed her like a man that would take my own life before I hurt her again. It was the kiss of a man who knew of no other woman and no other love. This kiss was the kiss of my biggest accomplishment.

From our first dance to the moment I carried Joya through the front door, I felt nothing but happiness. I laid her gently in the center of the rose petals scattered on the bed. The glow of candle flames filled the room and sparkles danced all over her body. I hovered over her, kissing her neck and caressing the curves of her hips, before I pulled her from the bed and turned her around. I sat down behind her and drew my finger slowly up her back, pulling the zipper down. She let the bodice fall into the ruffled organza skirt, showing a sheer corset and lace thong. As Joya mounted my lap, she pulled at my bowtie, releasing it from my neck, and teasing me as her lips softly touched mine. In the following moment, I cupped her behind and took her without hesitation.

The room spun into a new day before I'd realized what had happened. I loved watching Joya sleep but I was suddenly stricken with worry, and I wasn't exactly sure why. Yes, I had cheated on Joya and I wasn't proud of that. But that was water under the bridge now. I wasn't going to tell Joya because I wasn't going to mess up again. I just couldn't shake this feeling. After all, it was Diamond and she didn't bring nothing but trouble. For once in my life I had to be safe; I had to know.

I left Joya where she lay and drove to a walk-in clinic. I hated clinics. They were filled with ratchet freaks and wannabe thugs. It was embarrassing, but I stayed to myself and decided that if anyone asked I was getting a monthly test and I couldn't get in with my regular doctor. When they called me back, I kept my hood up, but I felt like I was walking the green mile. Was I walking to my death? Or would the governor call and let me live another day?

The room was cold and bright with that strong hospital smell I hate; like bodily fluids. I stared at the posters on the wall until the brown-skinned, female Dr. Fredericks walked in. She was carrying my chart and greeted me as she read.

"Mr...Adams?" she asked. I nodded my head nonchalantly.

"So according to this, you need a general STD test and an HIV test," she continued.

"I don't really *need* one, more like I just want to be safe. See, I just got married,"

"Well, congratulations. I'd think you'd already know each other's statuses before you decide to get married. But I'm not here to judge." She threw her hands up.

"What we'll do is take a urine sample and a blood sample. We'll check it for gonorrhea, chlamydia, HIV/AIDS, syphilis. We can't check for herpes unless you are actually having an outbreak. Do you have any reason to believe you might have herpes? Any sores, burning, itching?"

"Nah...I haven't had no symptoms of anything, I just like to be sure," I scoffed. I was embarrassed at what she must've thought of me. She probably thinks me and my wife are ho's; like we must have some kind of freaky open relationship or something. I just needed her to tell me that I was clean so I could get on with my life.

"Well, Mr. Adams, men don't often show symptoms until the disease has progressed, which is why it's so important to always use protection. But in any case, how about I get these samples so I can get you out of here," she smiled. After I gave her what she needed and I left her to the lab, my heart began to beat a little harder in my chest. I didn't want to go home and tell Joya that I had just come from getting tested. Then I would have to tell her why I needed to be tested after all the times we'd had sex. To avoid the conversation and provide myself an alibi, I stopped at Waffle House and picked her up a breakfast platter.

As I breathed in the spring air, I wasted no time rushing back into the house where Joya was still lying in bed, but staring at her cell phone. I slid across the bed as she looked up at me and smiled. Her face was still glowing, despite the exhausted fog in her eyes and her fading makeup. She sat up against the headboard and covered her naked body in the wrinkled sheets. The aroma of the food filled her nose as she grabbed at the styrofoam box in my hands.

"Is this food? I was wondering where you went," she started. I watched her inhale a sausage link before even grabbing the plastic fork from the bag.

"Hungry?" I asked sarcastically. Joya giggled, wiping the grease from her mouth while she finished chewing.

"Well, there's a reason for that," she said.

"What's that?"

"I'm pregnant," she confessed. The tone is her voice was almost timid as if she was a child who just got in trouble.

"Huh?" I replied. Everything was happening. But after losing the last one, I was disappointed to have missed the chance at having my own son; or daughter.

"However," Joya continued. "Here's the kicker. The little dot...was actually two,"

"Two?" I repeated what she said under my breath until I got it. "You mean twins?"

"Twins,"

"How did this happen?" I smiled. "*When* did this happen?"

"Well, I'm about nine weeks. You couldn't tell?"

"I mean, I thought you had a little pudge, but I wasn't going to say anything,"

"Smart move. Are you happy?"

"Baby, I couldn't be happier," I told her as I caressed her chin and kissed her. What I really wanted to do was scream it from the center of the Georgia Dome. Unlike most of these niggas, I was a father on purpose and not by accident. No, Joya and I hadn't planned on having kids just yet but we for damn sure weren't using condoms and she wasn't on the pill. Since her last pregnancy, we were okay with the thought of having a baby together. Now it was like making up for what we lost. I was already in love with them, and my spirit couldn't be broken.

15

I was getting a much-needed nap from suddenly having to put in thirty hours of overtime and feeling extra weak that day. My eyes popped open abruptly when I heard my phone ring. I sat up—feeling a little lightheaded but shaking it off—and took it from the nightstand, answering it.

"Hel—" I cleared my throat, "hello,"

"Yes, may I speak to Jayson Adams?" the woman said.

"You're speaking to him,"

"Mr. Adams, this is Dr. Fredericks. How are you?"

"Good, how are you?"

"I'm good. Listen, I've got your test results back and I was wondering if you were available to discuss them with me?" she told me. I forgot about those damn test results.

"Uh," I hesitated. "When were you thinking?"

"As soon as possible. Would you be able to come to my downtown office around three o'clock?" she asked. I looked at the clock on my phone. It was one-thirty. I had to be at work again at four.

"Um, yeah that's fine. What's the address?"

"It's 550 Peachtree Street, North East,"

"Alright, I'll see you then,"

"Great," she hung up. Here I am so damn happy that Joya is pregnant and I forgot that she might have to get tested too. I started praying then and there. I tried to convince myself that it wouldn't be as bad as I thought it might be. Maybe I just couldn't find the condom. Maybe Diamond threw it out afterwards. Maybe I flushed it and just don't remember. Maybe Diamond was actually clean and I'm worrying for nothing. These were big hopes with chances that were slim to none.

With the little time I had, I thought. If I wanted to know this bad I had to go to the source; the only person who had the answers to my questions. I pounded my head trying to remember a phone number that I'd tried so hard to forget. Then I dialed and hoped that it was right. It rang, and rang. This ain't the right one, I thought.

"Hello?" she answered. It was the right one.

"Diamond!" I popped up from the bed.

"Yeah, who the hell is this?"

"It's Jayson,"

"Huh, Jayson? Well, I guess Hell froze over. What can I do for you?"

"I think you've done enough already,"

"What the hell are you talking about?"

"Tell me what happened that night," I demanded. My heart was pounding and my frustration was slowly but surely rising.

"You gotta be more specific. What night?" she continued. The acting dumb thing was not helping.

"You know what night. I'm talking about the night me and my boys were at Magic City and I woke up in bed with you,"

"Oh," she giggled. "That night. Well, I think you can figure that part out,"

"What'd you do with the condom?"

"Nothing,"

"Why you lying? What, you save it? You trying to trap me?"

"No,"

"Tell me what you did with it!"

"I can't tell you what I did with it,"

"Why?"

"Because there was no condom!" she yelled. I went silent. A part of me already knew this, but another part of me wanted to believe that it wasn't true.

"Diamond, please tell me you're clean,"

"Why wouldn't I be?" she questioned sarcastically. I scoffed at the question and hung up. I covered my face with both hands. Diamond's response told me nothing. Why wouldn't she be clean? No, the better question is why *would* she be?

My stomach was beginning to turn; and the closer it got to three o'clock, the queasier I felt. By this time I was sitting in a slightly cushioned chair in front of an oak wood desk covered in neatly stacked paperwork. I ran my index finger up and down my leg; continuously scratching at my jeans and listening to the sound drown out reality. When Dr. Fredericks entered the room, my stomach dropped. I felt like, she could've told me I was clean over the phone. For her to have to see me as soon as possible must have meant I needed to get a shot for something.

I studied Dr. Fredericks' face to try and figure out how extreme the situation was. She was almost frowning as she read the documents in her hand. But that's as far as I could distinguish. What I did know is that the suspense was killing me; I just wished she would get on with it.

"Okay, so let's cut to the chase," she began. "All of your tests came back negative..." I breathed a sigh of relief. Finally, I could get on with my life and look forward to seeing my babies.

"Except for one," she finished. Soon I was holding my breath again. In the same moment I was confused and concerned all over again.

"What do you mean, all but one? Which one?" I wondered. She paused.

"Mr. Adams...we found AIDS in your blood work," she confessed. And just like that, my world and everything in it was killed. I thought I was going to be sick. As stupid as I've been in the past, this right here outweighed everything I could've possibly done and then some. I didn't want to hear anymore. Nothing else mattered. I was dead. To be honest, I'd rather have gotten Diamond pregnant; or even to have gotten something from her that was curable. But AIDS? AIDS was the king of all STDs and there was no way to move on from it. Even with HIV I might have had a chance. But AIDS took all my chances away.

I left Dr. Fredericks' office with six prescriptions and no more hopes or dreams for the future. The world moved in slow motion around me. The scenery blurred past me. I went deaf. My feet were heavy but I couldn't move the car. As my vision turned unsteady, my head fell into the steering wheel and I struggled to breathe. It was at that moment that I realized the life that I really lost was that of my family's. No wife, no babies, no hope for happiness. Now, outside of the hard part of dying, the even harder part is telling Joya. She's done with me for sure. And *till death* came a lot sooner than I had anticipated.

Once my quiet sobbing had stopped, I wasted no time calling Diamond. My fury had set in as it went over and over again in my head how this was all her fault. I couldn't understand how somebody could whore themselves out like she did and be happy about it. If she blatantly spread this shit around, she deserved to be shot straight through the forehead. My leg was shaking as I called.

"Jayson, two calls in one day?" Diamond answered.

"Bitch, you gave me AIDS!" I barked.

"What?! I don't have AIDS! Maybe it was that ratchet bitch you fuck with. She ain't no saint, trust me,"

"Fuck you, Diamond. You deserve the Hell you're on your way to. When you die, I hope it's slow...and painful," I hung up. When I threw the phone across the passenger's seat, I grabbed the wheel and started the car, taking off towards home. My anger is what got me out the car and onto the couch, but my hopeless depression is what halted my tongue when Joya ran through the door. She came in happily searching for me in a way I've probably never seen her.

"Hey, babe," Joya started. "I wanted to talk to you about something,"

"I want to talk to you too. Listen," I replied.

"I thought that, instead of us living here in *my* house—and we're definitely not living in your apartment with the babies coming—how about we just buy a new house, you know? We can start fresh with our new life and our family. What do you think?" she continued.

"Joya," I said lowly, taking her hands. "I need to tell you something,"

"What?"

"I went to the doctor the other day,"

"Why? What's wrong?" she asked. She stared at me lovingly

without knowing that I was about to send her whole world crashing down.

"Just know that I love you more than anybody I have ever known; and my vows were true,"

"Jayson, you're scaring me. Tell me what's going on,"

"They told me...that...somehow...I have AIDS," I admitted. Joya's eyes widened and her mouth opened as she took in a deep gasp of air towards the back of her throat. She froze until she could no longer hold her breath and slowly released it.

"AIDS? AI--," she swallowed. "Somehow? How the hell do you *somehow* get AIDS?"

"I wasn't myself, and I made a mistake,"

"Let me guess, you cheated on me with some random whore? Did you shoot up with a dirty needle? Have a blood transfusion? What?!"

"I'm so sorry, I was drunk," I explained. Joya snatched her hands from my grasp and backed away from me disgustingly.

"Joy," I restarted, "I didn't mean for any other this to happen. I didn't even know what was happening; I just woke up in the bed with the girl,"

"When?"

"It doesn't matter,"

"Jayson, when?" she demanded. Her voice was controlled but the volume rose.

"The night before the wedding,"

"Are you fucking kidding me? And you have the nerve to say your vows were true. I swear you love fucking more than you love me. Here I am, pregnant and I may not even get the chance to enjoy being a wife and a mother. Well, Jayson, thank you,"

"Thank you? For what?" I wondered. I was more than confused.

"Thank you for killing us all," she said as she walked out of the room and disappeared up the stairs.

Words like that pierce your heart in a way that it murders your soul. It was likely that I not only killed her body but I killed her spirit. It was bad enough Derek took her first child from her. But

I did something far worse by taking everything from her. This is the part when love makes you go really dumb. As I shoved my hands in my pockets, and sunk into my seat, I felt the crumpled bunch of prescription papers and wrapped my fist around them. I couldn't help but to think, why would I ever try and make an attempt at saving my own life? What did I have to look forward to? I just ripped everything I had out of my life. Joya was gone and my kids never even had a chance to live. Yeah, I gave up on my life the moment I heard the words *AIDS* and *YOU HAVE* paired together. I was done.

I was beginning to think my boss was getting the impression that I may have been dying. What he didn't know was that I actually was. That's the only reason I would call in every day for a week. What's a paycheck? I can't spend money when I'm dead. However, it was thoughts like this that made it dreadful waiting for Dr. Fredericks to come into the room. The lights seemed extra bright and I was so cold I was damn near shaking and covered with goose bumps. While my stomach was in knots, I found it much easier this day to keep from getting sick all over the place. I did feel weaker than usual, though.

"Jayson," Dr. Fredericks entered. Finally; I was starting to fall asleep in this meat freezer.

"How are we doing today?"
I hated it when doctors ask questions like they share a body with you.

"I'm straight," I said nonchalantly.

"Straight? Mm hm, okay step on the scale, please," she instructed. I hopped off the bed and onto the scale, focusing on the ceiling as she slid the markers back and forth. She wrote on her clipboard.

"I wouldn't say you're straight, Jayson, since you've lost ten pounds,"

"People lose weight, doc," I dismissed after sitting back on the table.

"Not in a week, and not safely. What's your diet like?"

"What diet?"

"What do you mean? Have you not been eating?"

"Well, you just dropped the bomb of all bombs on me a week ago and now my pregnant wife has left me. It's kind of hard to hit McDonald's on these types of circumstances,"

"Okay," she looked down. "I get it. But you still have to eat. Have you been taking your medicine?" she asked. I just cocked my head and pursed my lips.

"Jayson, come on, man. Are you just gonna watch yourself die? Is that what you're trying to do?" she wondered. I didn't move. "You're serious? Listen, I'm not here to judge you or the lifestyle you live. My job is to keep you healthy. If you're refusing to take your medication to be sure that you die, then I have no choice but to admit you for psychiatric evaluation and put you on a suicide watch,"

"Really? You gotta do all that?"

"I take my Hippocratic oath seriously," she shrugged. "I know it's rough; I can't imagine what it is you're going through. All I can do is help you through it. So, please help me help you. Eat, take your medicine. I don't want to look back on your case as a tragic story when there was something we could do about it,"

"You would really put me in the crazy house?"

"Psych ward, seventh floor, quick, fast, and in a hurry. Don't test me," she assured. I paused as I stared at the veins in my bare feet before slowly raising my head to respond.

"How...how am I supposed to feel taking care of myself knowing that I did this to my wife? And my kids? I don't even know them yet, and I'll never get to," I choked.

"Okay, Jayson, calm down. It's not even for sure that your wife has contracted anything," Dr. Fredericks commented.

"What?"

"Especially if she had fertilized eggs following intercourse, she may not even have it," she said. I couldn't believe what I was hearing. If this was true, everything that I thought the future

161

would be was a lie. There was still hope; hope that we could be together in the way that we'd always tried to be. Maybe we wouldn't fail this time. This changed everything. I had to tell Joya.

I ran home with a new outlook, just thinking about the *possibility* that Joya was okay. I burst through the door, screaming her name, but there was no answer; nothing had been moved from its rightful place which told me she hadn't packed up and left yet. As I shuffled through each room unable to find her, I decided to call her. I wasn't surprised when she didn't answer but I left a message anyway. Maybe if I told her the good news, she would actually hear me out. I waited for her, barely able to contain myself and praying that what Dr. Fredericks said was true. God, I hoped she didn't have it.

Night had fallen. Every clock read 10:17, and I wasn't sure anymore if she was even coming home. I started to feel low again. Joya was probably trying to figure out why she even married me in the first place. It's like I brought out the worst in her life. In the next moment, I heard the front door slam. I quickly bolted from my pacing spot behind the couch in the living room and greeted her long face. Without thinking, I hugged her tightly, but didn't feel her embrace me back. She felt colder than usual; which was unlikely due to the summer heat. I backed away from her slowly when I began talking.

"Joya, baby, listen. I talked to my doctor and she said you probably don't even have it," I started with excitement.

"Really?" she said distantly.

"Yeah. She said because your eggs were already fertilized, or something like that, you might not have it,"

"Interesting," she continued, piercing through my eyes with her stare. "Considering that I do, in fact, have AIDS and that there's a good chance I'll miscarry by my second trimester,"

"Oh my God," I froze. Joya proceeded to walk around me, dropping her purse and keys off onto the coffee table. I just couldn't move. I'd held onto this ounce of *maybe* all day and now it was gone. I didn't deserve to live past that moment.

"Jayson, come here," she asked. I heard her speak but I couldn't will myself to make a step. I felt, instead, as if I would drop right where I stood.

"Jayson," she repeated. I snapped out of my trance and, before I knew it, was standing next to her as she sat on the couch. I felt her grab my wrist and pull me next to her.

"I don't have anybody to help me through something like this. And you don't have anybody else except for your mom, and this might kill her," Joya admitted. She was somewhat right. The few friends I do have left probably wouldn't know how to handle it, and I hadn't even thought about my mother. She had just lost one child and it would've been her second and third grandchild dead.

"So, what are you saying, Joy?" I wondered.

"I'm saying...I don't want to go through this by myself and I know you don't. I probably should leave you, but I wouldn't be able to handle it. I'd kill myself first,"

"So, what does this mean?"

"It means...we stay married and pray that God keeps waking us up every day; and that he lets us have these babies," she said. Tears quickly filled her eyes. I pulled her to me without hesitation when she slowly gripped the back of my shoulders, placing her head into my chest. Joya wept heavily while I tightened my grip on her body. I kissed the top of her head and thanked God that He wouldn't let her walk away from me. At this point, I couldn't live without her, and I for damn sure didn't want to. There was no point.

Joya and I went to sleep that night declaring that we would try to live. We had gone through too much to go back now. It was as if this was the end of our road and we may as well go out together rather than quitting right before the last stop. The hardest part was choosing to keep up appearances. Joya and I had to keep working for as long as we could; pretending as if nothing had changed. We had to appear to be happily married as we prepared for the arrival of our twins. However, as each week passed us, it had gotten more and more difficult. Watching my mother fawn over ultrasound photos and buy baby clothes made it harder for us while accepting the fact that this may be as far it goes.

However, watching Joya's belly grow in size brought forth an interesting realization that it may be happening. We couldn't lose anybody else after all this; we were already hurting enough. She lay back on me in the bedroom as I massaged her bare stomach after an episode of vomiting that afternoon. Joya breathed heavily while holding her head and keeping her eyes closed. I suddenly felt a tap on my index finger. I lifted my head a little to look down over Joya's shoulder; she was nearly sleeping. There was another tap.

"Did you feel that?" I asked abruptly.

"Hm?" she answered, her eyes still closed.

"I said, did you feel that?"

"Feel what?" she asked. Another tap and she lifted herself.

"See, you felt that, though,"

"Hell yeah, I did. Oh my gosh," she smiled. "That's, like, our babies,"

"Yeah, it is," I agreed excitedly. It was in that spark of happiness that we forgot what was going on. We focused solely on the fact that she still had life growing inside of her. It made me wonder why we were acting as if they were already dead. Right then, they had let us know that they were alive and kicking. It was then I felt the overwhelming need to call my mom and let her know what happened.

"Mama, guess what? We just felt them move," I said the second she answered the phone.

"What?! That's so wonderful. How far along is she now? Three or Four months?"

"She's four. That's the first time we felt it though,"

"Oh, that's so sweet. I can't wait to feel that. I remember when I was pregnant with you; you never stopped moving through the whole thing. But listen, I'm glad you called. I've been meaning to tell you something,"

"What's up?"

"I met someone, and I wanted you all to come over so that you can meet him,"

"How long has this been going on?"

"A couple of months,"

"And I'm just now hearing about it?"

"Well, whose fault is that? You've been so distant lately; I haven't been able to really talk to you. Besides, I didn't want to say anything until I knew it was getting serious,"

"So it's getting serious, huh? I guess I'll come through and see what type of nigga this is,"

"Jayson,"

"Well, Mama, if I don't approve of this man then it ain't going down. I'm sorry. I'm not gonna watch you get played,"

"Tonight, six o'clock. I love you,"

"Aright, ma, love you too," I said before hanging up. "Baby, you think you'll be up for dinner at my mom's house a little later?"

"Yeah, I guess, whatever. I'm sure I'll be somewhat hungry by then, considering I probably won't eat until then," she replied.

"Ah, babe, you can't think like that. Didn't we say we would at least fight this thing? After this, I really think there's a good chance you'll have them,"

"I hope so, because I really wanna meet them," she cried. I held her a little tighter, wishing she could feel the way that I felt.

About thirty minutes to six, I came out of the bathroom in a pair of dark blue jeans, an aqua button-down shirt, and black Timberland boots. I had just dabbed on a bit of cologne when I noticed Joya still lay in the bed. She looked so depressed as she read a magazine and yanked the pages from right to left.

"Joya, baby, don't you think you should be getting dressed?" I asked her.

"For what?" she responded.

"Dinner...at my mom's,"

"Oh, I don't wanna go anymore,"

"What do you mean, you don't wanna go? It's just dinner at

my mom's. Come on, get up," I pled. I pulled her up out of bed and, as she stood in one stationary spot, I pulled a purple mini dress from the closet and started to take her shirt off.

"Jayson, I can get dressed by my damn self," she huffed, snatching the dress from my fingers and marching into the bathroom. Emerging a few minutes later, she was tugging on her dress complaining, "Jayson, I really don't want to go. I'm fat and I'm tired. And all she'll want to talk about is this pregnancy which is only going to remind of what is going on behind it. I can't do this,"

"Listen to me," I interjected, grabbing her shoulders. "You can. It's not that hard. We're just going to meet her new boyfriend and then we can come home. I can make all the conversations about him, maybe throw my sister in there somewhere, and that's it. I got you,"

"Jay, I don't know. I'm not really in the mood to be going out and meeting new people,"

"So, you're just gonna sit in the house and be miserable? I'm right here with you. I'm taking every step of every day right by your side. I know you don't want to lie to my mother but this isn't the time to tell her. I know it's hard to act like none of this is happening, but you have to be strong, okay? *We* have to be strong. This damn virus has me tired too, and I know you got it twice as rough because you're pregnant. But it's just a couple of hours. If it gets too bad, you can fake a sickness and we'll be out of there,"

"I might not have to fake it; which is what I'm afraid of,"

"Okay, calm down. If you start to feel sick, I mean really sick, just squeeze my hand or go to the bathroom,"

"Fine," she sighed.

We arrived at my mother's house right as the sunset kissed the sky, leaving orange footprints beneath the clouds. I pulled Joya out of the car and encouraged her to avoid acting as sickly as she was before opening the door. I walked in cautiously as I tried not to startle my mother but surprise her. The smell of her soul food penetrated the air and reminded me of Traycee and I running through the house as kids; I forgot how nauseous I really was.

"Smell that?" I whispered to Joya. "Are you still sure you don't want to eat anything?" She pursed her lips and nodded aggressively, almost with sarcasm. I held her hand as I followed the sounds of low conversation into the kitchen. I poked my head around the door opening and found my mother glowing over the stove with this bulky man behind her, whispering in her ear. I won't lie. This big, black, Ving Rhames-looking motherfucker was not somebody I was happy to see wrapped around my mama. The nigga looked like he had just gotten out of jail. And I know a thing or two about jail niggas. One of which that I didn't want one nowhere near my mama.

Most days she was dressed comfortably since she didn't get out much. But tonight, mama was snatched in a sleeveless, red dress with her hair curly and a full face of makeup. She was drinking a glass of wine as the two of them swayed in the same rhythm as she stirred. When I saw the tip of dude's tongue slither towards my mama's cheek, it was time to shut this whole shit down.

"Mama, mama!" I sang into the room. She slightly jumped as if I had startled her.

"Hey, baby," she smiled. She kissed me on the cheek before greeting Joya in the same manner. Mama gripped my hand and gently pulled me a few inches further into the kitchen.

"Son, this is Kirk. Kirk, this is Jayson and my daughter-in-law Joya," she introduced us. Joya linked her arm around mine, gripping my bicep. I gazed at dude and his blank expression. He held his chest out as he stepped around my mother to approach me. He wore a blue, collared shirt and khakis, but it was all so tight he looked like he was about to bust right through like the Hulk. I was hesitant and just waiting for a nigga to say the wrong thing.

"Jayson," Kirk started. "Good to finally meet you, son,"

"Likewise," I replied with a head-nod as he shook my hand, not taking his eyes off of me. I stared back into his dark eyes and squeezed his hand tighter. "Of course, I wish I could've met you sooner but, you know, my mom likes to keep secrets." There was a brief silence with the only audible sound being the boiling pots on the stove. Then a smirk shot across Kirk's face.

"Baby, I told you he could handle it," Kirk laughed.

"Handle what," I wondered.

"The news about us," he said, throwing his palm into my shoulder. The impact forced a violent cough to erupt through my chest. But I assured everyone that I was fine.

"Kirk," Mama interjected. "I didn't want to say anything until I was sure. As a matter of fact, before anybody says anything else I think we should eat. Look at Joya over there looking all frail. Don't be starving my grandbabies, now." Mama motioned Joya to the dining room where china was neatly placed around the table. Joya appeared exhausted like she was trying to force herself to even be present. I mean, I was definitely pushing through this night even though I was dying inside. But I couldn't let it show since this dinner wasn't really about us.

I followed behind to sit down next to Joya at the table.

"Babe," I whispered. "I know you feel like shit, believe me I do too, but could you try to be a little more upbeat?" She turned to face me and, without words, sent daggers through my face. "Okay, nevermind," I said. I thought it best to just take that loss and leave her alone.

I offered to help Mama set the food around the table and she accepted without hesitation. Bacon-wrapped chicken, mac and cheese, collard greens, and cornbread lit up the house in a symphony of smell that would wake a man up from a coma just to get a taste. Though my appetite was waning, I knew I would hate myself if I didn't get a piece of something. I fixed Joya's plate for her and made sure she had a big, frosty glass of water right next to her since that was probably the only thing she would touch anyway. I said grace over dinner before Mama looked around the table with a look of both happiness and being unfulfilled. Her smile was slightly dropped as though something had begun to take her mind away from the present moment. Kirk moved his hand over hers and gently squeezed it as he asked if she was okay. She looked at me and paused.

"I just wish your sister was here," she confessed. My head dropped for a moment and I stared at my lap. "She was always so happy for other people. I know she would be all over us with hugs and kisses right now,"

"I miss her too, Mama," I said in a low voice. Joya reached over and grabbed my hand as she sighed.

"Jayson," Mama continued abruptly. "We're getting married!" I paused like I needed my ears to do a double-take. What did she mean? I didn't know this nigga.

"What do you mean, Mama?" I asked, confused.

"Jayson," she sighed heavily and sat back in her chair. "I've been by myself for a long time now. And the second I got your sister back she was one again; and she's not coming back this time,"

"I get that but--"

"No, you don't. When you lose a child, that's a kind of loss you don't think you can come back from. It's like happiness doesn't exist anymore. I found my happiness again,"

"I'm just saying, this is just new. You don't think it's a little quick?"

"It's quick for you, not me. Life is short, son," Mama declared. I sat back in my chair and pursed my lips, moving my eyes in short glances around the room. My mama had that look on her face like she was unbothered and set in her decision; Kirk looked like he was just waiting for the conversation to be over; and Joya, Joya rested her head in her hand and squeezed her eyes shut as wetness fell through her lashes. When I asked her what was wrong, she shook her head and breathed sharply. She made a high-pitched wheezing sound as she inhaled before she began coughing. The hacking grew heavier as the tears dripped down her face and onto the plate. I tried to offer her water but she refused, wiping her hand across her nose and face. When she lifted her hand, her palm and face was covered in blood that was leaking from her nose. My mother and I jumped from the table to cover her face with napkins and hold her head back. Joya cried harder and began shaking. I kept telling her it was alright but what the hell did I know? Nothing.

16

Everything sounded so muffled; the nurses rushing and shouting around Joya and the rapid, inconsistent beeping of a heart monitor as they tried to get a reading on her pulse. She's hemorrhaging, they said. Joya moaned in pain and called out to me but no one would let me near her. I was still yelling to her it would be okay before I was forced out of the room. I didn't even know what was happening. My heart was pounding so hard it hurt.

I pushed back and attempted to get back to her when a nurse slammed the door in my face. Joya's shrill screaming of my name was the last thing I heard before the door closed. I threw my fist into the door when I felt hands pull me back and heard my mother's voice speak my name. All I could muster out was, "Fuck!" in a growl. I could barely breathe. I just knew she was losing the babies.

I sat on the floor outside of the room fidgeting like a crack-head. I was trying so hard to hear what was going on that I almost cussed out every person walking by. Then suddenly all the voices steadied. No one was rushing, no one was yelling. I hopped to my feet and pressed my face against the glass window, hoping some kind of sound would leave the room through the curtain and glass and reach my ears. I still couldn't hear anything clearly. Just then, the door opened and a woman in a blood-stained, white coat emerged, followed by nurses wheeling steel tables of used tools; their scrubs just as painted in blood as the doctor's. The doctor, a tall brunette with a strong face and a thin frame, breathed and wiped her forehead back and forth. I barely gave her a chance to speak before I asked what was going on. She breathed another sigh before she answered.

"We stopped the bleeding. But she did miscarry," she told me. I dropped my head and covered my mouth, whispering more saddened curses to myself.

"The good news is, she's going to make it and it looks like the other baby is too," she told me. The world stopped for a moment. I didn't know whether to cry or fall out. I put one hand on my hip and curled the other into a fist, holding it up to my mouth. I huffed through my nose, squeezed my eyes shut, and hunched over as silent tears fell across my face. My throat seized into a cough spasm and I felt hands on my back. As I regained my composure, I shook everything and everyone off as I demanded to see her.

"I wanna see my wife!" I barked. The doctor tried to stop me. She said Joya needed some time to get an IV and stabilize with oxygen. Then she told me they needed to prepare the room for guests and ya ya ya ya...My baby needs me. I scoffed at the doctor and pushed past her, entering the room. It was freezing and smelled of bodily fluids. The floor was decorated with droplets of blood and Joya lay back in the bed with an oxygen tube across her nose. The whoosh of the machine as it breathed into her made wish I could trade places with her. She didn't deserve this. I did.

The moment Joya turned her head and saw me standing there, she reached out with both arms and said my name. Her face was still streaked from crying and she sniffed as if she had never stopped. In two giant steps I was already at her side. I locked my arms around her while she sobbed into my shoulder.

"Oh, Jayson, it hurts so bad," she cried.

"I know, baby, I know. I'm here, I got you," I assured her.

"I thought it was happening. I thought I was dying,"

"I know, but you didn't. You're right here and I'm right here with you. And you still got life in you, baby. We still got one kicking in there,"

"One of them made it?" she wondered. The gleam of hope in her eyes almost brought me to my knees. She needed to still be able to have a baby more than I wanted her to. I kissed her face in several spots, just happy that she was still alive. Joya pressed her fingers into my face, unwilling to let me go. When I broke free from her grasp I grabbed a nearby chair and scooted as close as I could to the bed. I wasn't going to leave her. She was all I had. My whole world was lying in that hospital bed fighting to survive.

My mother inched her way into the room with Kirk trailing behind her. Her face dropped when she laid eyes on Joya in her current condition. She covered her mouth with her hand as she fought back tears.

"Oh, Joya," she cried. Mama moved around to the other side of the bed and hugged Joya tightly. "I'm so glad you're doing okay,"

"Yeah, my baby's a fighter," I said. I laced her fingers into mine and tried to read the heart monitor. I really didn't know what I was looking at but the beeps were steady and line was still going up and down, so that's all that mattered. Just then, the doctor pushed her way into the room looking quite disturbed with a set of papers in her hand. I hope this time she could tell me what the reason was for the miscarriage in the first place. She asked if she could speak to me alone but I refused. Anything she had to say to me she could say in front of my mama. Everybody in that room was all the family Joya had.

"Well, we got some unfortunate results back from your wife's labs," the doctor began.

"Unfortunate like what?" I asked. I stood to face her.

"Were you aware of your wife's AIDS status?"

"AIDS?!" Mama interjected loudly. "Jayson, what is she talking about?"

"Mama, please. Yes, I know about it,"

"Okay, well because the disease causes a poor immune system and she's pregnant, we've gotta get your wife on a round of fluids and medications a-sap. However, there is a chance that all of it could be too much for the baby,"

"So, what does that mean?"

"Your wife is very sick and very weak, Mr. Adams. We'll be lucky to get her strong enough to leave," she continued. I guess I already knew that the baby surviving at all would be a long shot. "And I know it's none of my business but if you haven't been tested, do so immediately. I'll put an order in to get her something for pain and nausea and see what all she can handle otherwise."

I turned slowly with my head towards the ground, not really sure what my next move
should be. I was scared. I felt like I took Joya's whole life away. To make matters worse, I couldn't sulk for too long since Mama yelled my name.

"Tell me what the hell she's talking about? Is it true?" Mama said. I nodded my head.

"Do you have it too?" I nodded again.

"Why didn't you say something?" she continued.

"How was I supposed to tell you, Ma?" I started to choke through my words and heavy
tears painted my face quickly. My leg began to shake nervously. "How was I supposed to tell you that you were about to lose another child? And it's all my fault?"

"Jayson, how did this happen?" Mama groaned.

"I fucked up, Mama," I said in a whisper. "I really fucked up. I deserve to be where she
is." Joya tried to speak up but I wouldn't let her. Mama wanted to convince me that I was being dramatic but I disagreed. We wouldn't have even been in this mess if I would've just controlled myself at the strip club. I shouldn't have even gone to the strip club. I should've just kept my ass home with my woman and everything would've been alright. But everything's not alright. It's fucked up beyond repair. I didn't need anybody telling me I wasn't the cause of it or that we could beat it. No need for anymore lies.

The only time I left Joya's side was the morning of Diamond's funeral. I randomly got a text from someone letting me know that it was happening. I don't know why but something in me felt like I needed to go. I showered in the room as usual. Joya was sleeping peacefully. Her heartbeat was steady and had been for the past few months since she was admitted. She was still fatigued most days but had enough strength and promise that she was no longer in as much pain, apart from a few small sores that had developed on her thigh. The baby was still growing but mostly due to a feeding tube that was placed in Joya's stomach. It was hard to accept any kind of hope but I was getting there.

I tiptoed out of Joya's room and left the hospital. It was a cloudy day. The sun was trying to shine but there was too much gray fog across the sky. I hopped in my car and stretched my seatbelt across my body, reaching in my pocket. I flicked my lighter and raised the the pack of Newport cigarettes to my lips, attaching one to the corner of mouth and inhaling. I never smoked cigarettes. But something about the cool flavor of the tobacco made me relax in the midst of all this craziness. I didn't want to be high in my last days so i chose to choose a vice that wouldn't alter my perspective. I wanted to be present for as long as I had left.

As I breathed and and felt smoke enter into my chest, I put the car in drive and headed to the church. I couldn't really fathom Diamond even stepping foot in a church. But I guess there was actually a side to her that people didn't see. Or at least that's how her family wanted it to be. When I stepped into the sanctuary quietly, I posted up the back wall. Looking around, there was only a handful of people in attendance; thirty, maybe forty, people. Everyone was in black and the room was so quiet that the pastor's voice echoed the room with every inflection. I watched past the benches and there she was. She lay in a mahogany casket with chrome handles. Even at a distance I could tell she was thinner than usual and her face was made up in natural hues. She didn't look like herself. Her soul was gone out of her and it was clear.

I listened to her mother talk about her in a way that was unfamiliar to me. She was a daughter who lost her way after trying

175

to raise her kids on her own. When she got hooked on cocaine just trying to make it through her jobs, she realized she could never take care of them and gave them to better families. But she was clean before she died. The girl actually had good intentions. It just looked like this life had finally caught up with her. Before I knew it, my eyes misted. It was time to get out of there. I snuck out just as quietly as I had come in and headed back to my wife.

When I saw Joya again she was awake watching *Cosby Show* reruns on the hospital TV. The color was draining from her face and her skin was blotchy. More sores had developed around her face and neck. Her chapped lips looked like scales and dark circles surrounded her eyes. Joya's once-full head of hair was now thinning with balding around her edges. I tried every day to tell her she was still beautiful even though she refused to accept it. I took my usual seat next to her bed and took her hand.

"You get some sleep?" I asked in a low, timid voice. She kept her view focused on the television as if I wasn't even there. After a few moments I placed my hand on her stomach and immediately noticed a difference.

"The baby died today," Joya said; her voice weak and mousy. I felt my heart plummet into my gut. I was only gone for a little while. How could it have happened so quickly? "I needed you and you weren't here,"

"I'm so sorry, baby. I should have been here, but I'm here now. Damn," I whispered. I clenched her hand tighter when she broke down into tears.

"I don't wanna live no more," she cried.

"Baby, don't say that!"

"No, Jayson! I love you so much. But it's over for me now. It's just a matter of time,"

"You still got time," I said. I lowered my head and lost the fight against my emotions. I was crying like a baby, begging Joya not to leave me just yet. We could go out together, hand in hand, on our terms.

"My time is up. Being in this hospital is just torture at this point. But I need you to know..." she paused. I lifted my head and stared into her milky eyes. "I really do forgive you for all of this." Joya pulled me close and held me. She cried in my shoulder while I balled in hers. I swear I was trying to be as strong as I could for her. I ignored my own pain and my own sores because I wanted her to know that she still had life. But as she wasted away she had decided that she'd rather submit to the inevitable. Fuck that! It wasn't over yet. Yes, the babies were gone but if she at least tried to get healthy we could have each other. She couldn't give up yet.

But she had. I sat by and watched Joya refuse to eat and vomit up her medication to the point that they forced it through her IV. Joya pulled the IV out of her arm on several occasions and removed the oxygen from her nose. Every day I asked her if she was sure, and tried to give her a reason to stay with me. And every day she stuck to her guns, giving me another reason why she had to let go. What I noticed, though, was that the moment before she took her last breath, she was at peace. I don't remember crying that day. By the time she was gone, I finally understood why she wanted it so badly. It was a release that she needed.

As I stand and stare at the base of Joya's gravesite tonight, I hold two newly-filled prescriptions in my pocket. It's colder than usual for a night in September. The only audible sounds are the crunching of sticks and leaves below my feet. There's not a person in sight. I'm not even supposed to be here but I snuck in. I take a few steps forward and sit down in front of the headstone, both of my legs on either side. I trace her name with my fingers, Joya Marie Adams. Even though she forgave me, I will never stop blaming myself for what I've done. I should have let her leave; go to New York far away from me so I could have never hurt her; so I could have never murdered her. I guess there's no use in dwelling on what will never be.

I take the bottles from my pocket and roll them through my hands, listening to the rattle of more than sixty pills go back and forth from cap to base. I unhinge the first bottle. These were supposed to manage my T-cell count. I pour them into my hand a few at a time and toss them down my throat. I always hated taking pills. With each handful, I feel the capsules struggle down my esophagus until I feel comfortable enough to take some more. With the first bottle successfully down, I start feeling a little woozy but I pop the cap on the second bottle anyway. These are the coated ones that were meant to keep me from producing too many white blood cells. Whatever; I repeat what I did the first time. I toss the bottles a few inches to the right of me and turn myself to lean my back against the headstone. With my arms resting on my raised knees, I wait. I close my eyes and wait for a darkness so deep that I know it can't be anywhere on this earth. I intentionally breathe a deep breath from the pit of my stomach to taste my love's final resting place. I hope she meets me there.

Electricity runs through my body like lightening and I start to see a light so bright I hope it means I'm dead. I tried to push out Joya's name as I wait for her to appear before me but I only hear other voices. I thought death was supposed to be quieter than this? What if Joya is trying to talk to me but I can't hear her because everybody's talking so loud? My body jolts upwards from my chest and I feel another electrical shock. *Clear!* It happens again. And again. I feel something down my throat, making it hard for me to speak. Suddenly, I feel like I'm throwing up with gallons of bile flowing through the tube from my mouth. It's painful. I thought you didn't feel pain when you die. They aggressively pull the apparatus from my throat and my vision starts to clear from the center. I try to sit up but I'm too weak and my stomach is on fire. I look to my left and my right. A heart monitor, IV, and a defibrillator. I look down. My shirt is torn down the middle and I'm lying on a stretcher. Motherfucker. I'm alive. I blow out a struggling breath of frustration and stare at the ceiling. I guess I'll have to try again.

CPSIA information can be obtained
at www.ICGtesting.com
Printed in the USA
LVHW041947061120
670968LV00003B/440

9 798646 199400